# ALL ALIENS LIKE BURGERS

# RUTH MASTERS

**All Aliens Like Burgers
by Ruth Masters**

First published 2010, re-published June 2023

© Ruth Masters

Originally published under the author's previous name, Ruth Wheeler

IBN: 979-8847577656

The right of Ruth Masters to be identified as the author of this work has been asserted by her in accordance with the Copyright, Designs and Patents Act 1988.

All rights reserved. No part of this publication may be reproduced, stored in or introduced into a retrieval system, or transmitted, in any form, or by any means (electronic, mechanical, photocopying, recording or otherwise) without the prior written permission of the publisher. Any person who does any unauthorised act in relation to this publication may be liable to criminal prosecution and civil claims for damages.

Cover by Tim Hirst

This book is sold subject to the condition that it shall not, by way of trade or otherwise, be lent, re-sold, hired out, or otherwise circulated without the publisher's prior consent in any form of binding or cover other than that in which it is published and without a similar condition including this condition being imposed on the subsequent purchaser.

For Mum & Dad

# CHAPTER 1

"What am I doing? What *am* I doing?" These were four words Tom Bowler often found himself asking. In this instance he was hopping from foot to foot, arms wrapped around himself in a bid to shield himself against the cool autumnal air. It was dark, it was late, and his favourite programme was on the television. Yet here he was shivering in the middle of a bitter cold rapeseed field. He flapped his arms around his torso, the sleeves of his jacket barely reaching his wrists, his face contorted against a sudden blast of wind. Tom looked at his watch. It was ten o' clock exactly.

Suddenly, an abrupt noise that sounded like a thousand hands producing one short, loud clap in unison startled him and he looked up. Tom's heart felt like it had jumped up to take a better view from his throat cavity as there, in the field, right in front of him, loomed an immense space craft.

The year was 1996 and one of the advertisements on the vacancies board in the Job centre had said simply: "Enthusiastic, bright, young individual to work in the catering industry at a local service station. No experience necessary as full training will be given. Good rates of pay."

It looked promising. Local was good. Every other vacancy Tom had perused that day had been either too far for him to travel, not yet having his own car, or they had required experience. How was he supposed to gain experience if no one would give him a chance to get any? He made a note of the details and made his way to the waiting area at the other end of the room. Tom Bowler had finished high school at eighteen years old with four A-levels. He had decided to defer university after thirteen years of education, much to his parents' disapproval. His parents had strongly advised Tom that if he was going to "switch off his brain" he should get paid to do it - however mundane the job may be. He suspected that they were hoping he'd soon get bored of earning minimum wage and be in more of a hurry to get back into the education system. Maybe he would, maybe he wouldn't, but as Tom waited - his right leg twitching nervously as he sat leant forward in the blue fabric-covered chair - the thought of earning some money brought a smile to his face.

"Next," came a nasal, female voice from behind a row of desks. Tom looked around and realised that it was his turn. He walked over to the desk, sat down and handed his job slip to a bored-looking middle-aged woman with short dyed-blonde hair and rounded glasses. Without even turning from her computer terminal to look at him, she took the slip from his hand, eyes affixed on the screen. She took his details, her adenoidal voice punctuating each question with an exaggerated rising intonation. Her vocal idiosyncrasies irritated Tom almost as much as the fact that she didn't turn to look at him once. The woman hastily tapped in a succession of digits, and read off the screen monotonically,

"OK Mr Bowler... interviews for this position will be taking place this evening. Would you like me to call the Managing Director for you right now to arrange one for you?" she was still looking at her monitor, seemingly clicking and scrolling down the screen with her mouse. "Yes please. If you don't mind," stammered the ever-polite Tom, a little unsure at the suddenness of the progression. Still without looking at him, she lifted her phone from its cradle and her nimble fingers danced over the keypad. He thought that the number seemed to be an awfully long one for an apparently local number.

"Hello, Mr John?" she whined into the telephone. "This is Veronica Hughes from the Job Centre. I have a Mr Tom Bowler here who is interested in the position you have advertised here with us. I understand that you are conducting interviews this evening?" There was a pause while the person on the other end spoke. Finally, she turned to face Tom "You're in luck. Mr John can see you at ten o' clock this evening. How does that sound?" Veronica asked, apparently unfazed by not only the rather strange name of the company's director, but by the extraordinarily unorthodox time of the interview. Tom assumed she was on autopilot and wouldn't notice if he had walked in there with three heads.

"Er... yes that's fine." "Yes Mr John, that time is suitable for the candidate. Do let us know how he gets on." She coolly replaced the handset. "Ten o' clock it is then Mr Bowler," Veronica smiled a forced congratulatory smile at him.

"Where do I have to go?"

A laser printer by the window behind her hummed into life as the words came out of his mouth. Veronica walked over to it and came back promptly with a sheet of paper which she handed to him. "Here are the details. Good luck." Seconds later, her eyes were once again glued to her monitor. "Next."

Tom read the printed address as he rode the bus home. He turned it over in his hands, curiously. He had read it correctly: "Top Field, Upper North Whitchall Park, Worcestershire." It seemed that the allocated time wasn't the only peculiar things about this interview. Surely an interview for a job at a service station would be held at an actual motorway junction service station. He had heard of interviews being conducted on neutral ground (he remembered how his cousin Max had once been delighted when he had found out that his interview for a job at a print company was to take place in his local pub), but this was ridiculous. A field in a park? Surely, Veronica Hughes would have thought something was amiss? Then Tom realised that that was unlikely, if the attitude he had witnessed this afternoon was any measure to go by. Grains of doubt were filtering into his mind – what kind of director of a legitimate company would want to meet candidates in a field at that time of night? Perhaps it wasn't legitimate? Or perhaps part of the induction was to have him scramble round an assault course, climb a few trees and test his fitness. But then, that wouldn't match the job description, unless it was related to character building training or a way of sorting candidates of a strong disposition, from the weak. And the advertisement did mention training would be given. Tom ran his hand through his crop of dark hair in deep thought. He pictured North Whitchall Park in his mind. He couldn't recall any buildings being near the perimeter, but he did remember that there was a public telephone box a few metres from the climbing frame in the play area. Perhaps if there was something dubious about the meeting, he could run to call for help in little over two minutes. He considered telling his parents about the location of the interview as a precaution, but he knew that if he did, they would never let him go. He was legally an adult, but Tom knew from experience how protective his parents could be. They would probably be right on this occasion, but curiosity now had its claws in him.

Tom folded the address slip and pushed it into his jeans pocket as he stood up to make his way off the bus.

"Cheers Henry," he said to the driver and stepped onto the street. He lived in a cul-de-sac in the next road in a quiet part of the suburbs of a small Worcestershire town. He had grown up in the district and knew the area very well. His parents both worked in managerial positions on an industrial estate at the opposite end of the town and Tom's school had been a few minutes' walk away. His cousin Max and his best friend Nathan lived nearby, so his immediate world was very small. He walked past rows of equidistant detached homes with their neatly manicured lawns. Each driveway boasted two or three shiny cars, few of which were older than three or four years. Once the bus had noisily pulled away and continued down the main road, the only sound he could hear as he turned into his close was birdsong and the sound of his own footsteps. Only his mother's silver Nissan was on the driveway; his father was probably working late again. He let himself into the house, the air fragrant with pine furniture polish.

"Hi mum," Tom called down the hallway as he grabbed the stairway banister and ran up the stairs three at a time.

"Hello dear," he heard her call cheerily from the lounge. Once upstairs, he crept into his parent's bedroom and used their bedside telephone to make a call.

"Max?"

"Hi Tom – 'you up to bud?" came back his cousin's friendly voice.

"'Right bud. Guess what? I've got an interview!"

"Yeah?" he heard Max stifle a laugh. "What's that for then? Computer games tester, you big geek?"

"No. And I think they take people's brains *out* to test computer games"

"I wouldn't mind getting paid to do it, mate!"

"Point made," Tom replied, "Anyway, the job I've seen n advert for is only for now – to get some work experience and some cash…but mainly to keep my parents off my back," he added. He told him about the interview. There was a short silence before Max's reaction came:

"Are you nuts?"

"Probably."

"What if the guy's some psycho and there is no job? I mean…it is a bit weird!"

"Well that's where you come in. I need you to stay by the phone just in case. If there's any sign of anything dodgy I'll leg it to the phone box and call you."

"And then what do you expect me to do, Tom? Tell your parents you went to meet this bloke at ten o' clock at night and get the rap for it?"

"No - I don't know exactly. Nathan's usually the one with all the good ideas but he's still on holiday, isn't he?" Tom paused, "I just thought someone should know anyway. I'm sure I'll be fine bud." He hoped he sounded confident.

"Well you can count on me – I wasn't planning on going out tonight anyway – catch you later bud."

"Later."

Tom went back to his own bedroom and looked through his wardrobe for something suitable to wear. He considered that while wellingtons would be suitable for trudging round a field, they wouldn't necessarily give the best first impression in an interview situation.

Tom's bedroom was of modest size, with a single bed along the far end of the wall, below a wide window. His curtains were ever drawn in order to shield the sunlight from his computer screen, which was on the wall opposite, surrounded by towers of games on dozens of floppy discs. His bookcase was crammed with science fiction and fantasy novels. There was also a shelf dedicated to his A-level coursework literature, now redundant to his requirements. A rack full of CDs and cassettes was along the adjacent wall, the music on them reflected in the many posters of alternative bands tacked to his blue and grey striped walls. He turned on his stereo as he liked to listen to music while he got changed and it helped relax him. Tom eventually opted for a pair of black trousers and a pale blue shirt. He thought that a tie was a little excessive for a seemingly informal meeting but shrugged on a matching jacket. He hadn't worn this attire in a while and so the jacket sleeves were a little short and his shirt cuffs were a little exposed, but he didn't have a lot of choice.

Four CDs and a cheese sandwich later, Tom stood in front of his bedroom mirror for a final self-inspection. He brushed breadcrumbs off his shirt and combed his hair down as neatly as it could, although he knew that it would look as unruly as ever by the time he got to the park.

"Bye mum, I'm just going to meet Max," he called as he descended the staircase, hoping that she wouldn't come into the hallway and wonder why he was going out without wearing his trademark jeans and hooded top for the first time in years.

# CHAPTER 2

Tom Bowler stood gaping, in awe of the colossal vessel, which had apparently come into existence in front of him. Menacingly silent in the dark field, the vast shape of the craft filled his vision. He ran his eyes over its exterior – a hull of deep granite black. A huge spherical central hub rested on an enormous, circular base. Six sturdy-looking tubes protruded from the sphere horizontally at equal intervals. The tubes, which Tom could only guess housed vast corridors, each led to a smaller sphere; black and substantial-looking. Three unrecognisable symbols, at least six feet in height, were positioned at the apex of the central sphere. The symbols were producing a soft purple glow, the only illumination apparent on the ship. Tom was unable to move, his heart thrashing against his insides. "What *am* I doing?"

"Well? Is he here?" Tyrander boomed abruptly.

"I'm just scanning sir… yes… yes I can see a human down there. Shall I let him in to see you?" Phelmer asked graciously. He often forgot that he was the captain of this ship when Tyrander was on board.

"From what I've heard about this unenlightened species, I don't think that he's going to have the courage to walk unguided through an open door into a spaceship. I think that he requires the *personal* approach." Tyrander said. There was an uncomfortable pause "Well?" he huffed, haughtily.

Phelmer looked at Tyrander who was sitting slothfully across from him in his flight chair, "You want *me* to go out and meet him?" Phelmer didn't wait for an answer, however and made his way swiftly towards a grey console on which rested a complicated-looking mechanism. Phelmer manipulated the apparatus with long, pale dextrous fingers until there was a loud popping, like the sound made in the ear when descending very rapidly. "Very well. Right-right. I will be back presently."

Tom was still looking at the huge symbols at the summit of the huge craft when a loud popping sound startled him. Coinciding with the sound, he saw that the symbols were no longer incomprehensible. Somehow their meaning was apparent to him: *"TSS"*. He thought they looked like some kind of

11

corporate logo, as if the craft was advertising the name of a business in the same way a company van would have an emblem adorned on the paintwork. This concept puzzled Tom so much so that he didn't notice one of the outer spheres slowly descend towards the base of the craft. The tube connecting the smaller sphere to the large central sphere flexed accommodatingly. From the corner of his eye, he saw a small figure exit through an opening and step onto the curved base. He watched the tube flex once more as the sphere rose again and re-aligned itself with the other five. Tom saw that the figure was walking towards him, illuminated only by a pale moon and the soft glow of the corporate logo. He watched in silent fascination, the only sound his thumping heart, fuelled by the adrenalin pumping round his system. He was frightened, but the lure of the situation and the puzzling vessel fed his curiosity and he craved an explanation. The figure was coming into the middle distance now, becoming more apparent. He squinted in the darkness in an effort to make out as much detail as he could. Tom could see that the figure was shorter than he was, but that its limbs seemed to be out of proportion with the body, two elongated arms swinging slightly with each step. The figure was slim in stature and effortless in gait as if it were gliding through silk. A single blue garment draped luxuriously to the floor, so that only the arms and head were visible. The fabric was tapered slightly at the waist and again above the legs, the initials TSS were adorned on the torso in violet and white. As the figure neared, Tom saw that it had a masculinity about him, although he didn't look like anyone he had ever met. His skin reminded Tom of the colour and texture of a foxglove, pale lilac with deep purple veins visible through the skin around his ears and neck. It was not that he thought of the individual as being grotesque, but he couldn't prevent himself from staring at him as he approached, politeness escaping him. Two hazel-green eyes were set beneath a large purple monobrow, although this was the only place hair grew on his head. A thin-lipped mouth widened into a smile and spoke.

"Greetings."

Tom was startled. It took him a while for his brain to comprehend that the individual in front of him was speaking to him - let alone that he could understand him. It took even longer for words to formulate on his tongue.

"Er… hello."

"Tom Bowler?" smiled the man.

"Yes," Tom cocked his head to one side, enquiringly. "Er… Mr. John?"

"What? Oh yes, I mean no. That's not even his real name, its Tyrander. I'm Phelmer." The thin purple lips smiled again, green eyes glinting. A look of realisation flashed across Phelmer's face as he reached into a pocket deep within the folds of his costume and revealed a small black device, the size of a notebook. He proceeded to touch it with one elongated finger, an orange glow emitting from it. Phelmer appeared to be reading something on the device. "Ah." Phelmer replaced the device in his pocket and held out his right hand as if to formally shake Tom by the hand. Tom responded. His lilac skin felt cool, but not unpleasant.

"Right. Right-right," Phelmer chirruped "to business. Would you like to follow me, Tom, so that we can commence the interview?"

"Er, yes." He said, his shaking voice betraying his effort to appear calm and composed. Tom found he was asking himself those four little words again - *what am I doing?*

"Right-right." He smiled and turned round, cloak billowing behind him.

"Are we going inside that sphere?" Tom ventured.

"Initially, but we don't conduct interviews on the bridge any longer. We have done so in the earlier transits for convenience, but we now have designated areas in these later models."

"Right" Tom responded, not really understanding. He followed Phelmer cautiously up over the slight arc of the base of the craft, the steady gradient curving slowly up towards the central hub sphere. Tom had forgotten how cold he was until they were several metres above the ground. He surreptitiously flattened his wind-swept hair with a moistened hand. They eventually reached the huge sphere. Tom looked up, but all he could see was the under-belly of the great orb jutting out above them. He was awestruck. Tom half expected Phelmer to open a hidden entrance with a wave of his arm, however he proceeded to lead Tom around the perimeter of the sphere until they came upon a large, robust door. It was granite black, thus complementing the rest of the ship, but obtruded a metre or so beyond the smooth edge of the globe. Phelmer reached once more in his pocket and pulled out a metal ring, upon which hung a large plastic emblem of the logo that glowed the same soft purple glow as the sign on the top of the ship.

*A strange, alien-looking key*, Tom presumed. Phelmer noticed him observe the emblem.

"Tacky key fob isn't it?" he smiled jovially and swung the key fob round the metal ring to reveal what looked like a simple door key. "Ah, here we are." Phelmer ran his hand over the right-hand side of the door, in the darkness, finally located a keyhole that would have best suited the door of a castle rather than a spaceship.

Tom bit his lip, the reality of the situation suddenly taking hold. He could run away now. He could run down the ship to the phone box, call Max and tell him what had happened. Most likely, Max would tell him he'd been watching too many science fiction films, but if he could convince him to come and see it, he was sure he'd be as amazed and fascinated as *he* was. If Nathan had been there, Tom suspected that he would have been inside the craft by now and looking for the flight deck, itching to take control.

"Well are you coming in, Tom? I was supposed to have begun the interview fifteen k... I mean, fifteen *minutes* ago." He seemed to be correcting himself. Phelmer politely held open the door for him. Tom stepped in. The heavy door closed behind them. They had entered a rectangular room, which resembled the reception area of a sparsely furnished down-market hotel. There was a desk in front of them, which wasn't manned, a strange variety of pot plant which Tom had never seen before and what Tom could only guess was a sort of unoccupied off-world hat stand. There were many doors leading off the lobby. The air inside the ship was comfortably warm, and there was a faint musty smell, usually reserved for libraries or city museums. Tom followed in Phelmer's graceful wake as he made his way to one of the doors to the left of the reception desk. If Tom didn't know otherwise, he would have insisted that he was inside a normal building on a normal street. But he seemed to be inside a hybrid of a revolutionary spaceship and a shabby bed and breakfast. He watched as Phelmer turned a conventional door handle and let him into another room. To his surprise, Phelmer stayed in the foyer area and closed the door once Tom had passed through.

"Ah, Mr. Bowler."

Tom turned around to face the direction of the voice, which had boomed at him. A large, rotund being was sitting rather awkwardly in what looked like an office swivel chair, behind a large, wooden desk. His complexion was pale lilac, comparable to that of Phelmer, and the only hair on his face was a bushy mono-brow which was cultivated above two piggy eyes on the globular face. Two long arms, like Phelmer's, rested on their elbows, lengthened fingers clasped together in a business-like manner. The differences between he and Phelmer, however, were marked. Tom guessed that this man was a good foot shorter than Phelmer and he was a great deal more corpulent around the middle. He didn't have the poised air, which Phelmer possessed, more an emanating superiority which filled the room. He radiated an impression of intimidation which Tom hadn't felt since he had last stood in the headmaster's office waiting for a punishment after mistakenly joining in with a lesson boycott. (He wasn't a rebellious pupil by nature, but he couldn't justify how a cross-country run in the snow was going to help him learn anything except how many bruises he could collect from repeatedly falling over on the icy ground.)

"Come right in, sit down," the being thundered. His heavy-lipped mouth grinned at him in a forced effort to appear amiable. But Tom couldn't help but feel overawed by the man's presence. Tom obediently sat in a rickety-looking chair opposite him, which creaked a little under his weight. All the preparatory advice he had ever been given about interview situations seemed inapt in this strange circumstance. He looked around the room, which was infinitely more pleasant than looking into the glaring eyes of the man sitting across the desk. They were sitting in a small office, again sparsely furnished. The walls were a dirty beige. There were no windows, but bright yellow light was secreting from a large desk lamp, emphasising the daunting ambience of the room.

"My name is Tyrander," said the corpulent man. Tom remembered his manners and faced him, forcing what he hoped was a confident, pleasant smile.

"Pleased to meet you, sir."

"Likewise," Tyrander beamed, a row of stumpy pale-yellow teeth peeking over his lower lip. "You are here for the position of Express Cuisine Attendant, that is correct?" but he didn't wait for a reply, "and as full training will be given, I don't need to see any relevant credentials. Your uniform will be supplied;

your working hours will be the standard four hours per rotation, seven rotations a week; wages will be transferred to you on the seventh rotation of the week - a rotation being a Truxxian day, in case you were not conversant with that. Any questions?"

"Er… are there any… rotations… off?" Tom hazarded. The prospect of a seven-day week was not a pleasant one, despite the ostensibly short shifts. Tyrander's eyes widened, then he seemed to be mentally calming himself, although his reply was as voluble as ever.

"I would have thought that the standard three rotations off out of every ten would be sufficient." To say Tom was confused was an understatement. Just where was this apparently local service station? "Any further questions?"

"Er, well there is one." Tom did not want to sound mal-informed or indeed presumptuous, but continued "Where will I be based? The advertisement said that it would be local." He was looking forward to hearing his explanation to this query.

To his surprise, Tyrander let out a guffaw. "Yes Mr. Bowler, Truxxe Superior Services is in close proximity to your galaxy. It lies merely between the galaxies of Triangulum and Andromeda. Hmm… perhaps I should give you some background information on the corporation as you are not as enlightened as I might have hoped." He shuffled down in his chair somewhat, although he still looked very uncomfortable and as if the chair might give way at any moment. He moistened his lips with a large, thick ashen tongue. "The planetoid Truxxe is the ideal location for ships - both commercial and leisure - which stop off on their long journeys between galaxies for fuel, provisions, sanitation, lodgings and the like. Because of Truxxe's unique location, it does not orbit a sun, however its energy is sourced from its thermal core, so we are magnificently independent." Two rows of yellow teeth grinned at him from his gleefully smug face as he rolled off his sales spiel. He continued in his deafening tone, "Truxxe is very rich in fuels - depending on the engine type of the particular craft, obviously. Incidentally, company transit ships like this one," he waved an arm in a general manner, "run on rapeseed oil which is ubiquitously available on Truxxe and, opportunely, a reason for landing in this field in particular." Another smug grin. "The craft is refuelling as we speak."

"I see. Great," Tom said. He was listening with some fascination, although the reality of the situation wasn't sinking in. A few weeks ago, he was taking his A-levels in the school sports hall. Now here he was, being interviewed by an alien being and being told about an inter-galactic space station where he had to opportunity to work as an *Express Cuisine Attendant*. The implications were mind-blowing and the questions rising in him were multiplying with each answer he received. He realised that the supposed interviewer had not actually asked Tom anything but had simply talked *at* him – this interview game was easy.

"I'm glad that you approve. I need to point out that due to the nature of the vocation, you will be provided with your own lodgings, which will be supplementary to your salary. So, you'll agree that this is a very attractive package that we're offering here, Mr. Bowler, in a very successful corporation."

Tom had not previously considered relocating to a new *town* for employment, let alone a different planet. But he admitted to himself that the prospect of such an adventure was very appealing to him, particularly when mentally comparing it to a mundane gap year spent in a dead-end job in his hometown.

"Am I to understand that you will accept the position, Mr. Bowler?" Tyrander's beady eyes glinted at him from within the flabby lilac folds of his round face, "I think that you are what we are looking for. Your scan reveals that you are a friendly, optimistic person with above average intelligence. You have all the qualities we are pursuing."

Scan? When was he scanned?

"Thank you," he said and before he could stop himself, ever the one to be persuaded by compliments. "Yes, I will be pleased to accept your offer."

"Good," he boomed. "Phelmer will show you out. I will send another transit ship to come and collect you in seven of your days' time. Ten pm." Tom stood up, feeling a little disorientated and rather perplexed by what was going to happen, but also relieved that he could return to normality again. He would be glad to get back home; it had been an inconceivably odd evening. He let himself out of the office and into the reception area once more where Phelmer was waiting for him.

"Well?" Phelmer said, bringing his face uncomfortably close to his own. "How did it go?"

"Well, I er… I got the job."

"Right-right. I knew you would Tom." He smiled and led the way back out of the ship and down towards the ground, back to where they had first met. "Until next week, then." He made to shake hands with him again, this time he didn't consult his pocketed device, but mistakenly held out his left hand. Tom followed suit and shook it with his own left hand. Tom opened his mouth to ask him if he was going to be met in the same place, here in the field, but before the words came out he heard a sound like a thousand hands producing one short, loud clap in unison and a sudden blast of air whooshed passed his face. The ship was gone. And so was Phelmer. Tom stood staring for a moment amongst the tall rapeseed plants, at the space where the vast craft had rested and refuelled. It seemed so unreal. It was still very dark and very late now, but Tom was not a bit tired. His mind was racing. *I've got to tell someone about this.* Tom turned and ran all the way to the telephone box by the play area, beyond the playing field. He hoped that Max was still awake as he breathlessly dropped fifty pence into the coin slot.

He dialled and waited for the ringing tone *Answer the phone Max.*

"Hello…" a sleepy voice croaked at the other end of the line.

"Max, it's me. You're not going to believe this…"

# CHAPTER 3

"It's the perfect scheme," Smirked Schlomm Putt, rubbing his hands together, malevolently. "And this time it will be in the perfect location, don't you agree?"

"It is a good plan" agreed Hannond.

"*Good?* It's *flawless*," he barked and gave a malicious grin.

"But, what happens if the Cuisine Attendants inform on us?"

"That's not going to happen, Hannond, because those unsuspecting burger boys won't even be aware of what they're doing."

"Perfect."

"Perfect, indeed."


"Tom, I thought you said that you saw this 'ship' disappear. What exactly do you expect to find?" asked Max, more than a hint of scepticism in his tone. They were cycling in the direction of the park. It was nine o'clock on the morning after Tom's encounter with Phelmer and Tyrander and Max wasn't happy about being woken up so early on a Saturday morning, especially after being woken up at close to midnight the previous night.

"Max, I've met with Aliens. Don't you get it? Don't you want to see where they landed their ship; a ship that I am going to be travelling in next week? - To another planet!" Tom panted, partly with exertion from pedalling so hard and partly with uncontained excitement.

"OK, OK. I'm not saying I don't believe you, but did we really have to get up so early?" Max complained.

"Oh, stop moaning, Max. You can tell Nathan all about it for me when he gets back from Majorca. He'll be so jealous you saw me leave in a flying saucer. I'll be well away by the time he gets home..."

"'Course you will, bud." Max shook his head in quiet disbelief at his cousin. They pedalled through the park and soon arrived at the rapeseed field; the bright, sun drenched view differing from the moonlit meadow Tom had stood in the night before. They came to a halt.

"So," said Max between short breaths. "Now what?"

"Look, look…" Tom dropped his bike into the deep yellow-flowered mass where it almost completely disappeared, covered by the crops. He ran forwards a few metres and knelt down. "They did use the rapeseed oil for fuel – look."

Max rolled his eyes and strode his way through the long stems after his cousin. "Don't tell me – crop circles."

"No, no, it's not the same," he protested. They examined the field. Before them, an immense circular patch of bare ground stretched, hundreds of metres across. "Look. They must have absorbed the rapeseed oil through the ship somehow; converted it into fuel or perhaps they just collected it up somehow and took it with them."

Max raised an eyebrow. "I've got to hand it to you, bud; this is one hell of a prank. In fact, it's almost a full-scale Nathanism if I ever saw one. You really are missing your best mate aren't you, Tom?"

"What? You don't believe me *now*, even after seeing this?" he stared at his cousin, looking from one eye to the other, desperately. "Look…if I had *somehow* cut all this rapeseed so thoroughly and so meticulously myself, where the hell would I have put it all? Do you think I hired a combine harvester?" he spat.

"Nothing surprises me bud, you have been pretty bored since leaving school. I think the pressure of all those exams have sent you a bit cuckoo." Max twirled his right index finger near his right temple to illustrate his point which only made Tom more frustrated and angry. "OK, OK I don't think you'd be *that* crazy, but come on. It *is* a lot to take in."

"I know," Tom nodded his head, still breathless. "I'm still having trouble with that myself." He looked again at the gigantic plot where the craft had been not twelve hours previously. "How do you think my mum and dad are going to take it?"

It was a week later, and Tom had spent the intervening time preparing himself both physically and mentally. He had found he had been unable to concentrate on anything for more than a few minutes - his mind was constantly distracted with thoughts of his new job. After dinner on Friday evening, his mother asked if they could sit and have a chat before Tom disappeared again.

"Tom, have you got a moment?" his mother placed a hand tenderly on his shoulder as he knelt down to put his plate in the dishwasher. Tom looked at his watch — five hours until he had to leave.

"I suppose so," he mumbled. He knew that he had left it late, but now would probably be a good opportunity to tell his parents that after tonight he might not be back home for a while.

"There you are again, always looking at the time and about to rush off somewhere." She led him to the lounge, his father in tow. The room was fragrant with a lavender scented air freshener. It was as clean and meticulous as ever. The television was switched off, accentuating the background tick of the antique wall clock at the far end of the room. They sat down on the plush white leather sofa, with Tom between them. His mother held his hand in both of hers, her painted fingernails clasped together. She looked into her son's eyes and Tom could see that a tear was threatening to form in the corner of one of her perfectly mascara-framed eyes. He saw her lips quiver just slightly as she opened them to speak, "Tom, dear... your father and I have noticed that... understandably, since you have got through the stress of your exams..."

"Tom" his father said sharply. Tom turned to face him, bewildered. "Have you been using drugs, Tom?"

"What?" Tom stood up and glared at his parents, looking from one to the other, gaping in sheer astonishment. "I can't believe you just said that! What do you think I..."?

"James!" his mother shrieked at his father and then looked at him once more with tender eyes, a distinct teardrop tumbling down her cheek. "Sit down, dear."

Shaken, Tom tentatively sat on the edge of his seat, utterly aghast. How could they think this of him?

"It's just that with your behaviour lately, we've hardly seen you this past week; you've been using the upstairs telephone and acting rather secretively. And all the time you've been spending out with Max since Nathan has been on holiday... has he been selling you something? He has always been the wild one of the family, I know." She cast the occasional glance at James, endeavouring to receive some of her husband's support. "I can't find half of your belongings — we presumed that you must be selling things to fund your habit. Are our suspicions correct, Tom? We won't be cross, we're just worried."

Tom sighed and tried to compose himself. "No, mum, I'm not on drugs." It was his turn to hold her hand, reassuringly.

"It's nothing like that. OK, I suppose I'd better tell you what's happening."

"I think that'd be a good idea." His father leant forward with interest. Tom took a deep breath. He had half-planned the story he was going to give his parents. He didn't want to lie too much, but he couldn't tell them the truth. *They really would think that I was on drugs then* he thought.

"I've found a job," he testified.

"That's wonderful!" he saw his mother's anxious face instantly transform into an expression of blissful relief. His father's face softened also.

"It's nothing to be too excited about - it's only a job serving food at a service station. The only thing is…I will have to live on site as it's so far away. That's why you haven't been able to find half of my things -I've packed a lot of my clothes and some books and things."

"How far away exactly?" his father asked, a tinge of apprehension in his voice.

"Er… Exeter."

"Exeter? Why would you want to live all the way down there?" his mother squeezed his hand slightly, her eyebrows arcing to an expression of concern.

"Well, it'll be good preparation for when I move away to University," he quickly replied. He was glad that he had picked somewhere in the same country, it needed to be as believable as possible.

His mother nodded, understandingly. "OK dear if that's what you want. When will you be going?"

"Tonight." Tom bit his lip, awaiting their response.

"*Tonight?*" gasped his mother. "Well… well how are you planning to get there?"

"I'm going down by train.," he said in matter-of fact tones.

"I can give you a lift to the station," his father offered quietly.

"Thanks dad, but I plan to travel around by bike when I'm down there so I'm going to cycle to the station. It won't take me long." Tom smiled and stood up, "I'll come down and say my goodbyes in a bit." He made to walk out of the room.

"I should think so too," his mother called after him playfully.

Tom packed some magazines for entertainment, plus a hand-held computer game and a pack of spare batteries. He didn't bother to pack any music because he didn't think the chance of an alien civilisation having a player, which played music on the formats he owned, was very likely and his nineties stereo was too large to pack. Tom scanned the room. He had no idea what to expect when he arrived, so how did he know what he would or wouldn't need? Thinking quickly, he went into the bathroom and removed two rolls of peach-coloured toilet roll from the long, chrome toilet roll stand. Then he opened the matching chrome bathroom cabinet and picked up his shaver. Pausing, he realised that he probably wouldn't be able to charge it anywhere and he doubted very much that even any of his parents' international connectors would be of any use anywhere he was going. He replaced the shaver and rummaged around the cabinet for a packet of disposable razors. *I wonder whether aliens shave?* He mused, as he piled the items onto a small white table near to him. Next, he grabbed his toothbrush, a full tube of toothpaste, a bar of soap, a face flannel and a small hand towel. He managed to wedge all of these items into a large hardwearing camouflage rucksack along with his pre-packed clothes and books. He was ready; physically at least. Tom had no doubt that he would look out of place on an alien world no matter what he was wearing so he decided that might as well be comfortable and decided on blue denim jeans and a dark hooded top.

At nine thirty, Tom made his inevitable farewells to his family, promised that he'd visit at his first opportunity, and wheeled his bike out of the garage. He took a deep breath and rode down the quiet twilit cul-de-sac in the direction of the park.

# CHAPTER 4

Schlomm Putt was pacing around the bridge of the Glorbian ship, The Cluock, his squat abdomen almost resting on his broad feet as he went. All he had to do was wait. But waiting was not a concept with which Schlomm was well accustomed.

"Hannond, check the orders," he bellowed

"Again? I only checked thirty krometres ago. We haven't had any orders all day."

"That's precisely the reason that you should keep checking," he spat. "They usually place an order on the tenth of the week."

Obediently, Hannond checked the cuboctahedron-shaped console in front of him. He rotated it until one of its square sides was facing him. Hannond touched the screen with a stubby grey finger. The console made a succession of noises before smugly stating that there were no new orders for meat products. He turned to Schlomm wearily. Schlomm shot Hannond an accusatory look despite the situation being no fault of his, then continued to pace.

Schlomm was ancient, in terms of his species, at sixty years old. He was barely three-feet tall and his almost naked grey body was covered in a sparse layer of wiry grey and auburn hairs. A pathetic sash of coarse dirt-caked material loosely preserved his dignity. His chunky feet were bare, save for a generous coating of unkempt auburn hair and each of his eight toes were crowned with a thick, brittle toenail. He wore a cantankerous expression on a greasy, jowly face. Hannond, however, was dressed comparatively smartly with his smooth, less filthy blue sash more liberally covering his body. The fine dark brown hair on his grey skin was somewhat well groomed. Hannond's large blue eyes complemented his mellow nature. He was Schlomm's younger, benevolent brother, and his easy-going nature meant that he was easily led, which had always been his downfall. He had come aboard the Cluock with his brother to continue his father's business in the meat delivery industry and to see more of the universe. But he hadn't bargained on being a part of the unlawful pursuits, which were customary of Schlomm's character. Schlomm was drawn by danger and illicit deeds, his quest for fortune being his greatest drive, no matter how ill gotten. He was prepared to risk almost anything and anyone and had no qualms about getting

Hannond involved. His confidence had inflated ten-fold since recently successfully having smuggled ten bags of gems out of his home planet to Spetula 7. But now he craved more to feed this new addiction; this was going to be the big one.

"Schlomm – TSS have placed an order," Hannond piped up from behind his console.

Schlomm grinned a large jowly grin and ceased his pacing; "Perfect."

Tom Bowler brought his bike to a halt and let it rest in the long stalks of the rapeseed plants. He hoisted his weighty rucksack higher up his back to prevent it from slipping. He stood well back; eyes fixed on the bare ground of the previous landing area in anticipation. He was breathless as he waited, staring intently.

"Hey, bud!"

Tom heard the rush of bike wheels through the field and Max's breaks screech to a stop.

"You're really going through with this then?" He dropped his bike and rested a warm hand on his cousin's shoulder while he got his breath back. Tom turned his back on the landing site and faced him.

"Of course I am. I've talked about nothing else all week."

"True." He swallowed and took a few deep breaths "Phew – I haven't pedalled that fast in a while…so what time's your er… lift?"

"In a couple of minutes." He smiled at Max. "You come to wave me off then? Or have you just come to see if I am making this entire thing up?"

"A bit of both really, bud." Max winced as Tom gave his shoulder a good-humoured punch. "When do you think you'll be back? Have they drawn up a contract or anything?" Max asked, rubbing his arm.

"I was too stunned to ask too many details at the time, Max. Although I have *plenty* of things I want to ask when I get on board – I've thought of nothing else. One thing I do know is that wherever I am going, they have ten-day long weeks. I get three days off a week and I only have to work four-hour days!" he beamed.

"Whoa!" Max's eyes widened. "Well, send me a post card if you can! Sounds like you'll have plenty of free time."

Again, the loud clamour of a thousand hands clapping sounded, as Tom had heard before, and Max's face was instantly illuminated by a pale purple glow. Tom spun round to face the direction of the noise and saw the craft's huge bulk towering above them; its abrupt appearance making its presence all the more startling. He heard Max gasp.

"I suppose th… this is your lift then, bud." Max was seemingly rooted to the spot, his eyes fixed on the great vessel before him, mouth open wide, utterly stupefied.

"Looks like it, yeah." Tom found that he was shaking. Now that the time had come, he wasn't sure how he was going to be able to deal with this. He had spent eighteen years in the same town, working hard at school, keeping his head down. And now here he was, about to leave the planet in an alien spacecraft and disappear into the cosmos. He was sure that his friend Nathan would be a more suitable candidate than he, being the adventurous type.

Tom watched as one of the ship's outer spheres made a slow descent towards the base of the craft on the end of its tube like a weighted flower head bending on its stalk towards the soil. He could make out a vertical slit of light widen into an opening in the granite black sphere, but this time no one emerged.

Tentatively he turned to Max, "Bye then, bud." Max lifted a hand in a laborious wave, his voice apparently having temporarily escaped him.

Tom hitched up his rucksack and strode up the curve of the ship's base in what he hoped was a confident manner. When he eventually reached the opening, he stepped right inside, attempting to look self-assured, but inside he was trembling with expectation and fear. He turned a final time to look at the small distant figure of his cousin. As the door closed just inches from his face, Tom realised that he had forgotten his bike.

Tom looked around him. The interior of the passageway in which he was standing was markedly different from the shabby wallpapered hotel lobby interior where the interview had taken place. It was still far from being pristine and ultramodern, Tom might have expected a ship interior to look, however. Soft white light was emitting from globes at equal intervals along the ceiling, each having the appearance of an illuminated crystal ball. A degree of effort had obviously been made to decorate the corridor - oval mirrored surfaces adorned the walls on either side of him, interspersed with ornate metallic emblems of the TSS logo. These embellishments could only dimly disguise the ship's obvious state of neglect, however. Tom could see several distinct streaks of brown rust running along the floor and ceiling and one or two of the mirrors were cracked. He could hear a faint humming, accompanied by a distant dripping sound. Occasionally one of the globed lights flickered eerily. *I'm surprised this thing can even get off the ground.*

"Please proceed along the corridor," a voice from nowhere startled him. He recognised it as belonging to Phelmer. He quickly composed himself in case the ship's crew was watching him, although he couldn't see anything that resembled a camera. "When you get to the double doors, go on through and turn right. Keep going until you reach another set of double doors, which lead to the centre of the sphere," echoed the disembodied voice. "There you will find the bridge."

Tom obediently advanced along the corridor, curious as to why the door on the main sphere hadn't been his entrance this time. He was faintly aware of the reflections of himself on either side of him, each time he passed a mirror, which made him feel ill at ease. He found that the doors were operated using simple door handles as they had in the other part of the ship. He followed the directions the incorporeal voice had given him until he reached the bridge doors. He took a deep breath and turned the handle of the right-hand door.

"Tom Bowler – do come in." Phelmer glided up to him holding out his left hand. He then corrected his action, apparently remembering, and switched hands. Tom shook his cold, lilac right hand politely. Phelmer was swathed in the blue robe he had worn when Tom had met him previously. He was baring his thin-lipped wide smile and the purple veins, which were spidering up from his neck and around his ears, were more apparent in the brightly illuminated bridge. "Welcome. Do take a seat – we should prepare for take-off." His green eyes were wide with enthusiasm as he designated one of flight chairs with his hand. Cautiously Tom made his way to the flight chair. It had evidently been made for people of Phelmer's kind, however, because the seat was high off the ground allowing for longer legs. The backrest seemed undersized in contrast, manufactured to support a much shorter torso. He dropped his rucksack onto the floor, jumped up and managed to perch on the edge before shuffling back into the seat awkwardly. He was attempting to position himself as comfortably as possible, when a wide black seat belt snaked its way across his lap and buckled itself in a contraption on the other side.

"Intellibelt." Phelmer informed him, triumphantly.

*It's a pity they don't have intellichairs* thought Tom as he squirmed gracelessly in the chair.

"Ready for take-off, Captain?" came a gruff voice. It was coming from the flight chair in front of him.

In his discomfort, Tom had barely noticed the other crewmembers. He had been vaguely aware of the presence of others had come into the room, but all his attention had been focussed on the face which was familiar to him. He struggled to look around from where he was sitting. There was an empty seat to his left and two manned chairs in front of him, facing a huge screen upon which was a view of North Whitchall Park. Phelmer sashayed over to the empty seat and eloquently sat down, arms aloft, allowing the intellibelt to slide elegantly over his lap. Tom saw that his feet were comfortably flat on the metallic floor, while his own swung inches above it like a toddler in a highchair.

"Right-right Pheo," Phelmer replied.

Tom heard the sudden loud clap once more, although the sound was much louder from inside the craft and it persisted to resonate in his ears for a few seconds afterwards. It did not feel to Tom as though they were moving however the huge screen now portrayed a boundless starscape. He gasped in awe.

# CHAPTER 5

"That was a smooth take off," said Phelmer, his huge grin radiating from his face. "Refreshments everyone?"

"The usual please, Captain," Pheo replied.

"The same for me Phelmsy," said the other helmsman pertly, his voice a little deeper than that of his crewmate.

"Tom?" Phelmer turned to Tom expectantly.

"Yes please. What's available?"

"We only have carbonated fruit water, or just plain water I'm afraid."

"The carbonated fruit water then please," he answered politely, guessing that he was referring to some kind of fizzy pop. Choosing water may have been the safer option, but Tom thought it sounded uninspired in contrast to his impending adventure. He was hardly sailing away in a pirate ship with a keg of rum, but it was close enough.

"Right-right." Phelmer allowed the intellibelt to retract fluidly across his lap, then stood up and cavorted across the bridge and through another set of double doors. Tom wondered why some things on the ship seemed so advanced, such as the intellibelts, yet all the doors, (the main door to the small sphere being the only observable exception) required manual operation. It was as if parts of it had been modified at a later date like a computer with several upgraded parts but with some obsolete programmes running. He looked around the bridge, as far as his constraint would allow. They were inside a huge, metallic spherical room. It was brightly lit, and a low desk ran around the perimeter; encrusted with lights, peculiar mechanisms and various monitors. Mercifully, the room was less shabby than the passageways and gave the impression of having a higher state of maintenance.

"Have you been to Truxxe before?" the deeper voiced helmsman activated a switch under his seat and spun round to face him. He had the resilient air of a lorry driver. If his complexion hadn't been so unlike that of a human, Tom could have sworn he could see a five o'clock shadow crawling across his face.

"Grenao, I don't think he's been on a *spaceship* before," Pheo mocked, without turning away from the screen. Pheo was pushing at buttons and tweaking dials. Tom felt his face flush.

He had thought he was making a good job of feigning that he was familiar with space travel, for he had not asked any of his burning questions.

"You *can* get up and walk around you know. You don't have to stay there now that we're out of your planet's immediate gravitational field." Grenao smiled pleasantly, rubbed his jaw with a long, broad hand, then rotated his seat and focussed his attention on the flight apparatus once more.

"How do I…?" Tom began and caught his breath as the intellibelt dutifully withdrew, rendering him free. Tom stood up cautiously and found that it was quite safe to walk around and made his way to the front of the bridge to get a better view of the screen. "How did we get up here so quickly?" he asked. His eyes were transfixed on the panorama of stars splayed across the screen. It didn't look real; it was as though he were watching a documentary on space on his parents' lounge plasma screen.

"We don't use the outmoded method of taking off with thrusters on these ships – uses up too much fuel," said Pheo. He coughed brusquely, his throat rattling in his next few breaths.

"Right, so how did…"

"Right-right, here we are then." Phelmer re-entered the room, seemingly hovering towards them, expertly balancing a drinks tray on one hand. He placed two tall cups in holders on the flight desk, which were conveniently positioned within easy reach of the helmsmen, but also safely out of the way of the instruments. He handed one of the tall containers to Tom, the liquid within it fizzing noisily. Tom took a cautious sip. The flavour was closest to tangy pear in nature. He found it instantly refreshing.

"How long will it take to get to Truxxe?" Tom asked Phelmer between sips. He looked at his watch and saw that it was almost eleven already.

"I don't think that contraption is going to be much use to you on Truxxe, Tom." His wide mouth tweaked into an even broader smile as he pointed at Tom's watch smugly. Why did everyone so conveniently avoid his questions? "It's late; I'll show you somewhere you can sleep for the remainder of the journey – bring your drink with you." He took a sip of his own frothing drink, turned and headed back out of the room. Tom hauled his rucksack onto his back and followed in his wake.

Phelmer lead him off the bridge and down a corridor much like the one he had passed through on entering the ship. They turned several corners until they reached a door on their left where Phelmer halted. He took a key from the folds of his robe with his free hand and handed it to Tom. "I'm sure that you will find it satisfactory. I will wake you when we arrive."

Tom let himself into the room. Now he really did feel as though he were in a hotel. The room was sparsely furnished, but comfortable. He was glad that the bed looked as though it would accommodate his shape more adequately than the flight chair had; a seven-foot long low platform covered by a thick royal blue mattress. The walls, ceiling and floor were bare metal save for a turquoise oval-shaped rug emblazoned with the ship's purple emblem. Instead of a window, an oval mirror with a hair-line crack across it, hung on the far wall. The room was lit by a single crystal ball globe above him. He took off his rucksack and lay down on the bed, realising how tired he was. All he could hear was the gentle hum of the ship's engine as he drifted off to sleep.

"Awaken, Tom."

Tom's eyes snapped open. A grinning Phelmer was standing by the bed. Tom looked at him, a little perplexed. The events from the previous evening had not been a dream. He wondered what the time was then remembered that the concept of the twenty-four-hour day no longer held its relevance. He then wondered why he had been given a key if the captain could violate his privacy and enter his room anyway. He sat up, groggily. He licked his parched lips and reached for the remainder of his drink, which was resting on the floor beside the bed. It refreshed him a little.

"Sleep well?"

"Yes. Thanks," Tom replied rather sleepily.

"Right-right. We have docked with the TSS port. If you would like to follow me once more, I will escort you off the ship and introduce you to your new supervisor."

Already? Tom was keen to visit an alien world, but he had wanted to explore the ship as well. He was arguably the first human to fly in an alien craft and he wanted to experience as much of it as possible.

"Can't I have a look round here first?" He picked up his rucksack, hopefully.

"What? Around the transit craft? Why would you want to do that? There is a whole new world out there for you Tom - aren't you keen to meet your new colleagues and settle into your new quarters?" But his question was obviously rhetorical because he was already making his way out of the door, expecting Tom to follow yet again. Tom hoped that his new colleagues were less infuriating than Phelmer. At first he had been in awe of him; everything from his remarkable appearance to his refined presence. He had appeared to be overly welcoming and polite, but in truth, Tom felt rather overlooked by him. Tom pursued Phelmer as he turned down the passageway. This time they headed away from the direction of the bridge and Tom was led through a labyrinth of passageways until they arrived at the tattered reception area. With his delicate, elongated hands, Phelmer heaved open the large door which led to outside the ship.

Once outside the ship, Tom gazed around while Phelmer matter-of-factly locked the door behind them. They had docked into a vast spaceport. Tom saw that they had parked on the end of a row of three other ships identical to the transit in which they had arrived. This served to make the once impressive-looking craft look almost commonplace, like one white Mercedes Benz parked next to another. Even this row of TSS transit crafts seemed dwarfed by the sheer size of some of the other spacecrafts and even more so by the gargantuan port. The port was incredibly noisy, with the sound of numerous ships docking and departing and the general hubbub of chattering passengers. Many beings were scuttling around the huge zone with luggage, packages and various belongings. Tom was amazed at the diversity of the visitors on Truxxe. He was startled to see that, apart from the occasional TSS employee in their blue robes, many of the visitors were wearing clothes similar to his own - particularly the ones who appeared to be leaving the station and boarding their ships. He wanted to laugh at some of the different shaped beings whose bodies were covered by denim apparel and black hooded sweaters. Tom was glad that he had chosen his outfit wisely (albeit unintentionally) so that he fit in quite well. He had only met one race thus far, but here were individuals of all shapes, sizes, colours and consistency. Some of them, Tom noticed, also seemed to be wearing complex-looking gear over their heads.

Phelmer followed Tom's gaze. "Fortunately, you do not require breathing apparatus as the atmosphere is the same as that on Earth." Phelmer said, as though he were reading from a guidebook. Tom realised that he had taken it for granted that Truxxe would have a breathable atmosphere. "This was taken into consideration when we advertised the position – it is preferable that our employees are used to a comparable amount of gravity, light, food etc. as us Truxxians. TSS recognises that failure to overlook these factors often results in the long-term discomfort of employees and so, quite understandably, they leave after a short while. Truxxe caters for all species of course, but for the inhabitants it is preferable that they can adapt easily to the environment here." And then he added, a little more colloquially, "*That* rule was difficult to get through the intergalactic diversity in the workplace laws I can tell you!" *And to think I was worried about a power point to charge my shave*r, Tom mused.

# CHAPTER 6

Phelmer's flowing footsteps escorted Tom Bowler across the vast spaceport. Tom continued to look around him as he walked, feeling like a dog on his first visit to the beach, lolling out its tongue and following its master. Everything was so *big*. There was *so* much to look at. Everything was so new to him.

The pair eventually arrived at a large archway through which dozens of other pedestrians were passing. They walked through a long, brightly lit foyer with a white tiled floor and twenty-foot high walls. An array of advertisement posters was displayed behind clear casing, interspersed with an assortment of direction signs: Express Cuisine Restaurant, Sanitation, Retail; they had walked right into the service station. They trailed through the populace and reached an area, which looked not unlike the kind of fast food outlet Tom had visited many times in his life.

Only this one was on a grander scale and the furniture was not identical. The purple chairs and tables appeared to be ergonomic; he watched as a tall, green creature, that reminded Tom of a praying mantis, made to sit down. A dark hood was pulled up over a green, insectile face in the manner of a masked assassin. He saw the purple globule beneath him adapt to accommodate his shape perfectly. In front of the being, the single central leg of an amethyst-coloured table lengthened so that it was at the correct height for his meal to be placed. The creature placed a cardboard container onto the table, swiftly unwrapped it with four dainty feelers and casually picked up what looked like a hamburger and proceeded to eat. Opposite him he saw another creature of the same species mimic these actions with an air of nonchalance. Such a startling scene was obviously of the every-day to these regular Truxxe visitors, Tom realised.

"The evening shift has just started by the looks of it." Phelmer broke his absorption in the unfamiliar surroundings. They walked through the row of tables and chairs to a door behind the counter. The door lead to a room, which Tom presumed was reserved for staff only. The furnishings consisted of a low, comfortable-looking corner settee, covered with well-worn purple fabric, a small table and what looked like a fridge. There was a viewing screen along the length of one of the walls, which was currently showing a still of the TSS logo. A Truxxian was sitting in the angle of the corner settee, his long feet resting lazily on the table in front of him. He was wearing a long blue robe, similar to the one Phelmer wore, but it looked a little less well looked after. He had a thick mono-brow, but, unlike Phelmer, he had a small crop of purple hair on his head. His foxglove-lilac skin was more radiant with fewer of the purple veins and he had an overall youthful appearance about him. His thin lips encircled a broad mouth with upturned corners generating a cheeky smile, and his blue eyes glinted under his mono-brow creating an overall mischievous looking effect.

"Raphyl," said Phelmer, the emphasis being on the first syllable, "meet your new colleague, Tom Bowler."

Raphyl stood up, confidently, "Hey Phelmer, what's a captain of a transit doing personnel's job for? You'll be flipping burgers with us next!" he said cheekily. Then he turned to Tom "Hey."

"Er... hey." Tom lifted a hand in a slight wave.

"Don't worry Phelms I can take over from here - the boss'll be on duty any krom, so I can introduce them and show him to his quarters."

"Right-right." Phelmer turned to Tom. "I'll leave you in Raphyl's capable hands then, Tom." He said simply and promptly left. Tom felt a little abandoned, but at the same time he was grateful to be in the care of someone of apparent proximity to his own age.

Raphyl sat back down heftily and threw his feet onto the table once more. Tom sat next to him, relieved to be finally free from the weight of his rucksack. ""So... *Tombola*? I don't know if the ALSID is working correctly, but that word translates as something you might play at a carnival or fete on some planets." He said.

Tom had, of course, heard this before. He knew the phonetics of his blighted namesake only too well. However, a smile crept across his face in realisation. "True – but so does yours, Raphyl."

"Really? My knowledge of other planets is obviously not as good as yours, Tombo," he said in a friendly manner.

"Er..." Tom decided not to correct him. "So, have you just finished your shift?"

"Yep," Raphyl grinned, relaxing further into the settee, contentedly. "Officially. Although I've been asked to stay late to look after the new kid." Tom looked at him blankly. "That's you, Tombo." He laughed.

"Oh right – thanks," Tom flushed self-consciously.

"Whoa how do you make your skin change colour like that?"

Tom felt his face redden even further as two intense, blue eyes inspected him. "That's clever – you're a strange species aren't you? Where are you from anyway?"

"Earth." Tom felt his face cool slightly as he realised that Raphyl didn't register his blushing as revealing embarrassment.

"Ah, in the Milky Way, right? I'm a Truxxian born and bred," he pointed to his chest complacently. "I've worked here for two phases – you'll pick it up soon enough. What's it like living in a solar system? Must be good to have neighbours."

"Well…"

The door behind Tom crashed open.

"Ah!" A thunderous voice interrupted their conversation. "Mr. Bowler!" Tom spun round to face the yellow-toothed grin of Tyrander, who undoubtedly knew how to make an entrance. "You made it all right then?" he bellowed. He rested a hand on Tom's shoulder, causing his knees to buckle under the load. "Ah, I see you have been put under the care of young Raphyl – hmm… don't let him lead you into any bad habits!" Tyrander beamed at the two of them then shuffled his great purple bulk through the small room and out of the door on the opposite wall.

"You met the boss then?"

"Tyrander interviewed me, yes."

"Don't worry – we don't see much of him. He doesn't come down to the shop floor much; he prefers to laze about in his office. Raphyl jabbed a long thumb in the direction of the door through which Tyrander had left. "All the offices are through there – we're not supposed to go past this point generally but I expect you will be once Miss Lolah arrives."

"Miss Lolah?" It sounded to Tom like the type of name that might be associated with an exotic dancer.

"Our supervisor. I must warn you though…" his words trailed off as if he had sensed something. Tom thought he felt something too although he couldn't justify the sensation. A moment later the door to the restaurant swung open and a six-foot-high robot strode into the room. It was covered with bronze-coloured casing and looked as though it had been crudely cut to form a basic Truxxian shape, with a short body and long, metallic utensil-like limbs. On its head was a single camera lens where you would expect the eyes to be with a purple fabricated expressionless mono-brow above it. A black grilled speaker was formed into a fixed smile across an angular face. It wore a blue peaked cap and a matching TSS robe had been loosely hung round its boxy torso. The overall effect was quite startling. Tom was startled still when it spoke; a soft, alluring female voice emitting from its black grill.

"Hello, you must be Tom." Tom felt a shiver go down his spine at the sound of this entity saying his name.

"Hi," he said nervously. He couldn't understand why he found this unsophisticated looking appliance so enticing. It was so obviously a machine, and it wasn't only the voice that had him captivated; Tom found that he was utterly transfixed by her presence. He found himself running his eyes over her metallic face and to where her robe met her long, bronze neck.

"Would you like to go on through to my office then Tom and we can begin your induction?" Her permanent features remained expressionless, but the words reached Tom's eardrums like the softest touch of silk. He willingly stepped forward and made to open the door which lead to the offices, however he felt clammy skin under his hand instead of the cool of the metal door handle as he realised Raphyl had beat him to it. Raphyl smirked as he opened the door to allow Miss Lolah through.

"There you go Miss Lolah," he said triumphantly.

"Why thank you Raphyl," she whispered at the beaming Raphyl and stepped through on her awkward metallic legs. Why did Tom feel so jealous about that small gesture? And over a robot? He was so confused about what he was feeling, but he couldn't bring himself round to thinking clearly. He followed her through the door and along a blue and lilac corridor until they came to her office, which was decorated using the same palette of colours. Once inside, he took a seat opposite the robot across a huge amethyst desk. He was so mesmerised by her that he didn't even mind the uncomfortable low-backed, high-legged Truxxian chair on which he was sitting. He wouldn't have minded never moving again if he could be in the company of the incredible Miss Lolah. He realised that he was gaping, rather impolitely, at her. But she didn't seem to mind in so far as a robot can portray emotion with a fixed expression. Her tone was as soothing and serene as ever.

"Tom, are you aware of your duties as an Express Cuisine Attendant?"

"Well I haven't been given any details," he replied honestly, his eyes set on her camera lens.

"OK. Well essentially you will be working closely with Raphyl, whom you have already met, for the first few shifts. Then you should be competent enough to work by yourself. I'm sure you'll pick it up quite quickly." Tom was hanging on every word that secreted so beautifully from the black speaker. "Your duties, to begin with, will be taking customer food orders and keying them through so that the chefs can process them." He knew that the fundamentals of the job were mundane, but her words made the role seem fascinating as Tom digested each delightful sentence. "Eventually you may wish to switch roles occasionally and take a turn with the food preparation, although you will need further training for that and it's still early rotations yet. As you may have been told, you will be required to work four hours per rotation. I don't expect that Tyrander would have explained to you that our clock works on a decimalised system so therefore a rotation is ten hours. This may come as a shock to you, coming from Earth, but your body clock will soon adjust." Tom comprehended, through his hypnotised haze, that working four hours out of every ten was going to be exigent, but at this moment this did not faze him. He could be told that he had to stand on his hands in a furnace for a week and he would still have the unperturbed look of tranquil adoration on his face. "You will have three rotations off a week and I'm sure Raphyl will introduce you to the station's leisure activities available for your free time." She paused.

"Fantastic." Tom smiled, agreeably.

Miss Lolah's camera lens made a crude whirring noise as it focussed in on Tom.

"I think the next thing on the agenda is to get you into a uniform." Tom flushed at the thought of her getting him in or out of any clothing. Then he tried to take control of his thoughts. *It's a robot. A machine. A thing. Stop thinking of it in that way - I never thought like this about our toaster.* He struggled to be in charge of his emotions. Why did his heart skip a beat when her lens had centred in on him? He watched as she stood up and strode ungainly up to a metallic lilac cupboard, with her strange robotic walk. She opened it with a clumsy jerk and took out a folded robe, with a blue cap placed on top. She placed the garments on the desk in front of him with a jolt. "Please wear these while you are on duty. If you wish to purchase any clothes for your recreational time, I'm sure Raphyl will show you around our many retail outlets on the station."

"Thanks." He picked up the outfit, eyes still transfixed on Miss Lolah.

"Thank you, Tom. If there are any problems or if you have any questions, do come and see me. As your supervisor, I will be around during your shifts anyway." After a pause, she added, "I'm sure that Raphyl is keen to go off duty now if you would like to go and join him. I'm sure you're eager to get settled into your quarters." Tom saw this as his cue to leave and so he hesitantly stood up and made his way out, unwillingly taking his eyes off the robot. Strangely, by the time he had reached the far end of the corridor, he felt normal again. In fact, he was ashamed to think about the emotions he had been feeling in the presence of the supervisor robot. He couldn't explain the state of arousal he had felt in her company – she was a poorly constructed metallic parody of an otherworldly being. How could he have possibly found her attractive even for a second, let alone feel so captivated by her and so willing to please? The closest Tom had ever felt to this, was the morning after a somewhat heavy evening involving too many lagers and a girl who looked like Godzilla's uglier sister. He cringed at the memory as he re-entered the staff room. Raphyl was still sprawled out across the corner settee.

"She got to you good and proper didn't she?"

"What do you mean?" Tom was taken aback.

"Don't worry, Tombo, she got to me too. And after two phases of working under her, I still get mesmerised."

"What do you mean?" Tom asked again, taking a seat beside him.

"The Supervisor – she's a Pherobot."

"She's a *what?*"

"A Pherobot. A strong pheromone field surrounds her. If you are in the vicinity of that field, then you come under their effects. And they are far from subtle as you have probably experienced!"

"Hang on, you mean she is like a kind of Siren?"

"I'm not sure what you're talking about Tombo, but all I know is that when she's around, all the males in the area respond to her. It can be a problem because it makes us competitive - did you see how we were both compelled to open the door for her? For an ugly metal *box?*"

"Right…" Tom was trying to grasp the concept. "But *why?*"

"Why? Because healthy competition within a workplace is encouraged. Most companies have Pherobots in managerial positions. They suppress rebellious behaviour and make employees more eager to please – and eager to work harder."

Tom gaped at him.

"You mean they take away our free will?"

"You can look at it that way I suppose, yeah." Raphyl shrugged

Tom was astounded. He felt used. He felt that his emotions had been violated.

"Hey, women have been doing this to us males since time began – this is just a little more… intense".

Tom nodded, comprehending.

"Well," Raphyl stood up slowly. "Only nine and a half hours until our shift starts so I'd better show you where you're going to be sleeping".

# CHAPTER 7

Hannond Putt was hauling six crates of meat burgers into the loading bay of The Cluock. He was sure that this was a bad idea. It was true that the adrenalin-fuelled excursion, which had resulted from their previous exploit had been exciting, but he had also felt a great sense of relief when it had been over. Schlomm, on the other hand, was obviously still riding on this thrill before any feeling of good judgment had chance to wash over him. And again, it was Hannond who actually ended up doing all the groundwork. As he worked, Hannond mentally went over the plans again. It would be like last time but on a grander scale.

Schlomm had made the *discovery* quite by accident, two phases ago, after picnicking with his brother Hannond on the distant planet Spetula VII in the M32 galaxy while trying to impress two of the planet's female inhabitants. He hadn't prepared the feast himself, of course, but had assigned Hannond to put together a lunch of meat, sliced root vegetables and a deceptively strong alcoholic beverage. The picnic had been unsuccessful as far as romantic issues were concerned - however the brothers were compensated, by the *discovery*. Hannond cringed at the memory of the manner in which their dates had behaved. The two petite, pretty females had devoured their share of the meal, before he and Schlomm had barely begun, and then proceeded to fall asleep before the wine had even been uncorked. At first the pair thought that they had inadvertently managed to poison the women and had made to leave. But these were the days when their collective knowledge and research on otherworldly beings was limited. Spetulans digested food only when they slept and so their behaviour was conventional on Spetula VII. Hannond had observed that the women were still breathing and so they had made an agreement to stay with them at least until they awoke. Long after Schlomm and Hannond had consumed their share of the feast and had a dozen themselves, the women had asked to use their ship's facilities as it was conveniently parked nearby. On their return they had politely thanked the brothers for the meal and promptly left. Disheartened, Schlomm and Hannond Putt had watched them leave and returned to their ship.

What the ill-informed siblings were also unaware of was that the Spetulans' leaving in this manner was also a customary signal that they would return to the same spot five rotations later for a second date and for their second course. Five rotations later, the females had returned to mournfully find the picnic spot vacant and vowed never to date Glorbians again.

Meanwhile, Schlomm had spotted something sparkling from the bottom of the defecation cylinder on the ship's sanitation deck. Glorbians, with their squat bodies, stumpy legs and widely set feet, had no need for a high toilet bowl and so simply stood over one of these cylinders which plummeted into the bowels of the ship. The stench was highly potent but Glorbians are accustomed to this way of living and are not easily repulsed. Schlomm could just about detect a precious orange glimmer amidst the murk, metres below. His eyes widened as he recognised the unmistakable aura of a Glorbian gem.

Schlomm had mentally traced back through recent events to try to deduce how this gem had resulted in being in the defecation cylinder of his ship. He had wanted to keep his findings to himself, but after hours of pondering in circles he had enlisted on his brother's help. Between them they had worked out the origins of the discovery. Prior to preparing the picnic, Hannond had been planting gem crystals in the poor soil of Glorb and there had evidently been an accretion of them on his hands - Glorbians were not famous for their personal hygiene. While it was not impossible to cultivate Glorbian gems on their planet of origin, Glorb's deficient soil meant that the process was slow and laborious and the unpredictability of the climate meant that what was reaped was often a great deal less than what was sown. Additionally, as the crystals were so profuse on Glorb, the final produce was nonetheless worthless. (Many Glorbians who grew gems from crystals did so mainly for the gratification of having achieved something – the gems were also characteristically striking to look at). But there, in The Cluock toilet, was a fully-grown Glorbian Gem.

There on, it didn't take Schlomm long to concoct a plan to smuggle gems freely through Truxxe's service station. Their father's business already benefited from existing customers on the planet, so they used these as an intermediary to get the meat, laced with gem crystals, onto the planet. The crystals were small enough not to be noticed - even a stray seed from a sesame bun would be huge by comparison. Opportunely they could be detected by neither taste nor smell and so the whole procedure would go unnoticed. The ingenious nature of the Glorbian gem crystals, they had discovered, was that once they were ingested by certain carbon-based life forms, the most significant part of the process would begin. Acids in the body would break down the molecules of the crystals, which was the first part of the process. Then natural mineral accumulation in the body along with traces of magnesium and iron would form the basic compound from which the indigestible crystals could germinate. Over the intervening hours as the body processed the bulk of the foodstuff, the crystals would have the perfect conditions in which to cultivate. Then, by the time the gem crystals had matured, they would be in that most disgusting of places; the TSS cesspool. Hannond had to applaud Schlomm – the plan was inspired. After all, Glorb was abundant with gem crystals and to say that there was an intergalactic market for the jewels was an understatement. He only wished that their own digestive systems had the same effect on the crystals; they would have to consume huge quantities to achieve the desired amount. The quantity of visitors to Truxxe was astronomical – an unsuspecting production line of visitors.

So now the crates were all loaded into the bay. They were ready to be delivered. And all Hannond needed to do was apply for a job in Truxxe's Superior Services sewer.

Tom followed Raphyl's lazy amble out of the staff room, across the busy restaurant and to the foyer through which he and Phelmer had walked a little earlier. They came to a lift. Raphyl pushed a circular button on the wall adjacent to it. The door hummed open to reveal a surprisingly spacious area which would have accommodated twenty or thirty humans. The lift was empty, however, and once inside Tom saw what looked like a palm-sized track ball recessed into the smooth white interior wall where you might expect the button panel to be. There was an arrow in the centre of the ball and numbers from zero to forty ran around the perimeter in bass relief on a gold surround. Raphyl placed a hand on the ball and rotated it slightly so that the arrow pointed to the number thirty-two.

"Most of the lodgings are on floor thirty-two," Raphyl informed him. "At this end you've got most of the burger boys.

That includes us and anyone else who works in Express Cuisine – cleaners, chefs, attendants, the caretaker."

"What's on all the other floors?" Tom felt a bit queasy – originating from a small suburb, he wasn't used to travelling in fast moving lifts in high constructions. He felt that the trip on the TSS transit craft had been smoother by comparison.

"More living quarters, admin offices, recreation floors, storage, all sorts," he replied, stifling a yawn. The lift doors opened, and they looked out onto a long corridor, which stretched so far that it looked as though the walls met at a point somewhere in the distance. Tom couldn't quite comprehend the immensity of the place. There were a few other workers milling about; some of them were wearing the corporate robes, others, strangely, looked as though they shopped at the same place as Tom. The walls were clinical white save for a scrawled message along a section of the left-hand wall. It looked as though it was someone's initials rendered in fluorescent paint, BB. As they walked past, however, Tom heard a soft sucking sound and saw the writing slowly fade away until it looked as though it was never there, revealing just pristine white wall.

"Anti-graffiti paint," Raphyl said, noticing Tom's look of perplexity.

"Right…"

"I think I know whose tag that was, but it's a bit of a waste of paint if you ask me – only lasts a few kroms. I admire his determination though."

Tom nodded absently and continued to follow Raphyl until they came to a white metal door with the number twenty-one printed in blue halfway down.

"Er…looks like this one's yours. I forgot to give you this." Raphyl took a key from the folds of his robe and handed it to Tom. "I'll let you settle in a bit as it's your first night. I'll show you round some of the rec places tomorrow if you like. Bit tired now, I'm afraid."

"OK. Thanks, Raphyl. Um…what happens in the morning, where do I go and what time? I don't exactly have a clock for here – I only have my Earth watch."

"Just make your way down to the staff room in the morning. Don't worry about waking up on time – you won't oversleep." Raphyl gave him a friendly smile and continued down the corridor. "See you tomorrow, Tombo."

*More unanswered questions* thought Tom as he turned the key in
the lock.

His accommodation was simple but inviting to the weary traveller. In the main room there was a single bed, a storage cupboard and what looked like a cooking area. There was also a dining table and chairs made from the same material as the furniture in the restaurant. He sat down on one of the chars and was amused by the strange sensation he experienced as it morphed compliantly around his frame. It was soon moulded perfectly to accommodate him. He shifted in his seat and the substance shifted accordingly. He was so comfortable that he fell asleep where he was.

**Paaaaaaaaaaaaaaaarp!**

Tom awoke with a jolt. What on Earth was that? It took him a while to remember that he *wasn't* on Earth and he gulped. His heart was racing from the intensity of the blaring alarm.

**Paaaaaaaaaaaaaaaarp!**

*Raphyl was right,* he thought as he put his hands over his ears. *How could anyone sleep through that?* He realised that the sound was coming from a speaker high up on the wall. When he was certain that it wasn't going to sound again, he tentatively removed his hands from the sides of his head. His heart was still pounding from the shock. He didn't know how long he had before his shift began, but Tom ventured through one of the doors which led off the main room in an attempt to find a bathroom. He found himself in a good-sized en-suite, painted in a pale blue like the rest of his apartment. There was a large tub with several taps aiming into it; he surmised that the one with a red cap was for hot water; that the blue cap was cold; but he didn't want to think about what the green, yellow and orange capped taps might be piped to. *I expect they have to cater for all species,* he mused. He raised an eyebrow in horror when he realised that the strange-shaped toilet was made from the same morphing material as the chairs.

Once he had finished in the bathroom, he inspected himself in the apartment's only mirror which ran from ceiling to floor. He felt rather smothered in the long blue robe, let alone ridiculous. He had decided to wear shorts underneath because he just didn't feel right without something on his legs. The cap fitted him perfectly at least, his crop of dark hair poking out the bottom all the way around. He wondered how they had got his measurements then shuddered as he remembered that they had scanned his brain without his knowing to ascertain his personality profile. Perhaps they had done the same with his body? Tom tried not to think about it. He was here now. An employee on an alien planet. Far from home. He suddenly felt very alone. He had no idea where on the floor his colleague Raphyl lived and he was currently the closest thing he had to a friend. He thought about Max and Nathan and wondered what each of them was doing, what his parents were doing. He wondered what time of day it was on Earth, what was on television. He thought about all the simple things he was beginning to miss already. Just how far away from home was he? *Pull yourself together Tom. This is an* adventure. *Just think how many people would want to be in my position, with their mundane lives on Earth.* He tried to assure himself. He became conscious that he didn't have time to feel anxious and, checking he had his door key, made his way down to the staff room.

As Tom approached the staff room he felt a familiar sensation. *Miss Lolah,* he thought. *She must be in there.* Sure enough, when Tom entered the room he was greeted by the bizarre looking mechanical alien, Raphyl and three other employees whom he had never met.

"Good morning, Tom," said Miss Lolah in her alluring, convincingly feminine tone. "Everyone, this is Tom Bowler who is our new Express Cuisine attendant. Tom, this is Maytey Reeston, he keeps the place spotless for us."

A man with an orange complexion and a long, wiry body contorted his face into an expression, which looked to Tom like a grimace, although he suspected it was the way he smiled. Tom greeted him politely.

"And these are our chefs. This is Jephle - I take it you already know that Truxxians don't have surnames?" she turned to Tom.

"No, I didn't know."

"Well now you do," she said pleasantly. "Jephle is a little shy, but a remarkable cook. That's why he puts his skills to practice behind the scenes." Jephle looked like and older version of Raphyl but held himself uneasily as if he were a little overwhelmed by the attention. He forced a reticent smile in Tom's direction. "And this is Jambole Farr," Miss Lolah continued. The other chef was a portly-looking lizard-skinned person with wide yellow eyes, which darted about in every direction before settling on Tom's face. He looked rather odd, to Tom, in his blue uniform and his cap was a little ill fitting.

"Ah, young blood!" Jambole's voice was unexpectedly loud and his tone startled Tom.

"Jambole is not quite as shy!" Miss Lolah added.

"Nice to meet you Tom." Jambole's eyes darted to Miss Lolah where they prolonged their glare. He saw that Jambole must also have been under the pherobot's influence.

"Raphyl, remember that you are to let Tom shadow you today. Tom, I trust that you will be all right. Any problems, I'll be in my office. I'm glad to see that you look so smart in your uniform". Tom blushed unnecessarily. He didn't expect a robot would have a concept of smartness of appearance. Someone opened the door behind him, and a girl walked in, dressed in uniform. He was glad that he wasn't last to arrive on his first day.

"Good morning, Kayleesh." Miss Lolah said to her. "Kayleesh, this is Tom Bowler. Tom, Kayleesh is also an Express Cuisine attendant." Tom was vaguely aware of the girl's appreciative grin, although he felt the pull of Miss Lolah's effect on his emotions and found it hard to steer his thoughts from the robot.

"Right, now that you're all here, please get to work." said Miss Lolah and headed in the direction of the offices.

There were no moans of complaint as Tom might have expected, in effect everyone obligingly left the staff room and took their posts in the restaurant. By the time Tom had followed Raphyl to the counter area, he was safely out of reach of the effect of the pheromone field. Now that he was out of the pherobot's simulated influence he noticed Kayleesh properly for the first time. He wanted to go over and speak to her as she busied herself with a stack of food cartons, but Raphyl was behind him.

"Hey, Tombo."

"Hi Raphyl."

"You *do* look so smart." Raphyl jested, his indolent grin stretching from ear to ear.

Tom laughed. "She doesn't hang around the whole time then?"

"Who? Miss Lolah? Not all the time, no, thankfully. She does make you want to work hard to impress her, but it can also be quite distracting having her around if you know what I mean. Bit of a contradiction really – it's an old system." Tom nodded.

"What does that mean?"

"What?"

"When you move your head like that?"

"Oh," Tom laughed. "It means 'yes'."

"Oh." A look of bewilderment on Raphyl's face morphed into understanding. Tom liked the fact that he was doing the teaching rather than the learning for once.

"Are you skiving already, Raphyl?" It was Kayleesh. She was trying to tear some cellophane wrapping with her teeth.

"Kayleesh – do you know what this means?" Raphyl proceeded to nod. The serious expression on his face as he did this made the two of them laugh.

"Of course I do, it means yes," giggled Kayleesh.

"Oh," Raphyl looked a little nonplussed.

"You're from Earth aren't you?" she asked Tom.

"Yes. Er... are you?"

Kayleesh giggled again "No, I'm from much further than the Milky Way. I'm from Augtopia".

"Sounds nice."

"You wouldn't say that if you'd been there." She said ambiguously. Tom saw that Kayleesh looked remarkably human, save for a few subtle differences. Her twinkling, playful eyes were deep violet and her dainty teeth were uniform in size and structure. She had an almost elfin disposition, with delicate ears, which he noticed tapered at the top. Her eyes, although large, were slightly skewed. Other than these distinctions, her complexion was a shade paler that his own and she was near enough the same height as him, maybe an inch taller making her six feet tall. Her long, golden hair flowed down to her shoulders and her proportions were similar that of a young human woman. Her tapered robe boasted a small waist and embellished her curvy hips. Tom guessed that she was about eighteen years old, although he couldn't be certain of how Augtopians aged and was too courteous to ask. Tom realised that he had been staring at her and, blushing slightly, turned to Raphyl.

"What's first then, boss?" he joked.

"Just follow me as Miss Lolah said. It looks like Maytey Reeston's just opened up."

Tom saw that several customers had entered the restaurant area. They were in two groups who sat down at separate tables. One person from each group walked over to the counter to place their orders. One was one of the jeans-wearing praying-mantis creatures Tom had seen the previous day and the other was an exceptionally short dark-skinned man with a preposterous amount of blue hair. Kayleesh went to serve the praying mantis and the other customer approached Raphyl's sale point. The till, Tom saw, was a complex looking console. There was a screen and an assortment of buttons.

"I'd like to order four burgers please." The man was too short to see over the counter. All Tom could see from where he stood was the summit of his blue curls. A dark hand reached up and placed some yellow pieces of paper next to the till. Tom found the scene so amusing that his shoulders began to shake. He bit his lip in an effort to control himself.

"Would you like anything else?" Raphyl said routinely.

"No thank you, just the burgers," came the reply.

"I'll do this slowly so you can follow," Raphyl said to Tom. Tom watched as Raphyl ran his hands rapidly over several of the keys.

"W… wait Raphyl – what did you do then? That was too fast."

Raphyl chuckled "I was just logging in, don't panic. *Now* I will process the order. Tom saw the screen burst into life and was relieved to see that the till was operated using a simple touch screen process. Raphyl cycled through several of the items on the screen which were displayed in picture form. An image of a burger in a bun scrolled across the screen and he pressed it four times. Next he pushed a green button on the keypad. The price flashed on the screen: six D. To Tom's surprise, a hole yawned open on the counter where the customer had placed his money and swallowed it.

"Three burgers." Tom recognised the voluble tone of Jambole Farr from the kitchen area. Kayleesh walked over to the blue shelving behind them and collected the order for her customer. She placed them onto a tray along with three cardboard cups. The praying mantis creature thanked her and walked away with the tray. "Four burgers." Jambole called. Raphyl responded, although with less enthusiasm than his colleague. He took the burgers from the shelving, murmured a 'thanks' to the chef and placed them on a tray. Two hands reached up and took hold of the tray and the customer carried it aloft, his blue locks almost knocking the food off the tray as he went.

"So... this touch screen till. It looks pretty easy." Tom didn't want to patronise his new friend, but he felt compelled to mention the obvious simplicity of the system.

"It is," Raphyl grinned.

"So... if it's just a case of touching the pictures of the items and pushing the green button, couldn't the customer do it themselves? I mean, the money side is taken care of too by the looks of it".

"Yes."

"Er..."

"Yes, you're right. The customers could do it themselves. Even their change is deposited in a hatch on the other side of the counter, so we don't even have to worry about that," he chortled.

"So... why do we need to be here? *Why can't* they do it themselves?"

"Ssh... you want to keep your job don't you?" Raphyl whispered with a wink.

"Of course, I'm just curious."

"The answer's simple – it's the personal touch. Customers don't want to be served by a robot or a machine. They like the old-fashioned approach."

"Fair enough," He shrugged. "And another thing..."

"Go on," Raphyl said sleepily. He was leaning on the counter. Tom didn't think that he ever stood up straight.

"Well, burgers. Surely different species like different food – how come the main food we sell is burgers?"

"You're right, different species do like different food. But come on Tombo, *everybody* likes burgers."

"Well, what kind of meat is it?"

"Who cares? Who knows if it's even meat?"

Tom decided not to continue on this line of enquiry, but there were still so many questions flying round his head.

"OK, what about the currency? What is 'six D' and will everyone passing through the service station have them?"

"D stands for denomination. And no, they don't have it. It's not even Truxxian currency - it's purely used at TSS. There are coin exchange points in the docking areas where customers substitute their currency for Ds. Kind of like tokens. Didn't you change your Earth money for Ds when you arrived?"

"No. I didn't really think about it to be honest."

"Ah. Well, don't worry, your wages will be in Ds anyway."

Tom wanted to ask how much they got paid but he saw another customer approach the till and decided to discontinue his questions for the time being.

# CHAPTER 8

Tom continued to watch how Raphyl and Kayleesh worked for the remainder of the shift. He estimated that the four Truxxian hours was about six Earth hours, because he was quite hungry by the end of his shift. He could rely on his stomach to be a good indicator of what time it was. Tom observed that Kayleesh was a much more dedicated worker than Raphyl, with whose apathetic temperament would make a sloth look athletic. Regardless of the monotony of the job, Kayleesh seemed to run on pure enthusiasm. She was consistently polite to customers and always seemed gratified. He wondered why he had been asked to shadow Raphyl and not Kayleesh. Tom presumed that perhaps Miss Lolah had calculated that shadowing a member of the opposite sex would prove too much of a distraction. And she would have been right.   The restaurant had gotten quite busy at one point during the day. Tom wasn't sure if this had been lunch time, but the artificial lighting in the building had been at its brightest. By the end of the shift it was as if it were twilight, with a soft glow illuminating the restaurant. After work, the employees each helped themselves to a complimentary burger. The taste reminded Tom of warm luncheon meat, although the texture was pretty similar to that of a beef burger. Even so, he was glad to wash it down with a free carton of fizzy drink - whatever flavour *that* was supposed to have been. After they had eaten, Raphyl offered to take Tom to one of the outlets to buy him some recreational clothing.

"You can pay me back on pay day," he said. "I'd rather that than walk around with you in your work clothes – or worse, your Earth clothes." Raphyl shielded his eyes and laughed.

"What do you mean?" Tom asked, perplexed "my clothes are perfect for here, surely? Everyone here seems a bit fashion-victimish wearing the same thing and everything, but at least I fit in here."

Raphyl shot him look of sympathy "You don't know then, obviously."   "I don't know what?"

"That you stick out like a stewberry in a ruffleberry bush."

"Er..."

"Let *me* explain." Kayleesh appeared between the two of them. "The reason that you see everyone wearing similar clothes to you, Tom, is that the suits that people are wearing are releasing a virtual Wardrobian Effect."

"A *what?*" Tom nearly exploded. "Are you joking? Because I've already been scanned without realising it at least once, I've been under the influence of a pheromone field and *now* you're telling me that even *clothes* have something sinister about them!"

"They're not sinister. The inbuilt scopes in these outfits are just influencing the sensory part of your brain," Kayleesh explained. "The scope judges what each visitor – or employee – considers as normal dress and directs their thinking so that they view everyone as they'd feel most comfortable. It's all in aid of ensuring harmony and reassurance on the station." Tom thought that Kayleesh sounded like Phelmer with her formal vocabulary - would Tom also sound like a walking advertisement for TSS once he had been working there for a while? Tom looked at Kayleesh and then at Raphyl.

"But that…that doesn't make sense! Why? Then how come I can see the uniforms then? They're different from what I see the visitors wearing."

"So the visitors can tell us apart of course. They know who's on duty and who isn't," said Raphyl, simply.

"This is one strange place." Raphyl looked a little offended, but Tom's pursuit for answers was too strong for apologies "OK…If that is the case then wouldn't it be better – more *reassuring* – if instead of seeing all these different species and races, that I saw everyone as looking like me? Like human?"

Raphyl's sombre expression was suddenly over-ridden with a huge Raphyl smile, "and you think *we're* strange!" and he began to laugh.

"And a little racist," said Kayleesh, curly. "The wardrobian effect is only built into compsuits. Everyone who works here has them for recreational time and most of the people who pass through here buy them too – but, mainly for souvenirs to be honest."

"Right. So where do I get one of these compsuits from then?"

"I'll show you," said Raphyl. Tom followed him for a minute or two until they arrived at a clothing outlet. Raphyl stopped and pointed up at the sign above the shop door, *Unifit*. Tom followed his friend inside and they were confronted with several rails of clothes. It reminded Tom of a shop he had once visited on a beach holiday, which sold only wetsuits. Tom thumbed through one of the racks. The garments were all-in-one generic-looking costumes in TSS blue, baring the purple logo on the left breast.

"They're all the same, Tom," Raphyl grinned, knowingly. "They all look as though they'd fit your kind because they do. They fit anyone. It's the nature of the compsuit. Pick any and change through there." He gestured towards a curtained-off section of the shop. Tom obeyed and unhooked one of the suits. He found it surprisingly light as he carried it towards the changing area.

*What am I doing?* Tom took a deep breath then changed out of his uniform, took off his shorts and stepped into the compsuit. He pulled the fabric up over his hips, stomach and chest and inserted his arms into the sleeves just like an extremely light-weight wetsuit. At first it felt uncomfortable and felt compelled to rip It off, but as he went to fasten the suit at the neck, he caught sight of himself in the mirror. He gasped as the reflection showed him wearing a pair of brand-new blue jeans and a black hooded top with The Red Hot Chilli Peppers, his favourite band, printed on the front. *Excellent.* He looked down at himself and the illusion was still present. Amazingly, Tom also felt comfortable now that the suit was fastened; the substance felt like soft fabric on his skin. He beamed as he exited the changing room and was greeted by Raphyl's look of approval.

"That's much better."

"Great." He found the experience of shopping with another male a surreal enough event in itself but buying clothes had never been like this before. He realised that he would never have to go shopping again now that he had a compsuit, and he was glad about that fact when he heard the cost.

"It's going to cost half of your wages, Tombo. The material they're made from isn't cheap." Raphyl said a little solemnly as they approached the cashier. "You still want to buy one?"

Tom hesitated. "Er...well I don't really have a choice – if I'm going to be around for a while I should make an effort to fit in."

Raphyl smiled "OK then. Oh, and while we're here, you might as well buy a timepiece. Just get a cheap one, they don't cost a lot anyway." Without waiting for an answer, Raphyl unhooked a wristband from a small rack on the serving counter.

Once they had left the shop, Raphyl lead the way to the recreational level. Tom studied the timepiece around his wrist. It would take some getting used to. The decagonal face had a number in each of its ten segments; one being at the top where he would expect the twelve to be on an ordinary clock face. Each slice was illuminated in green to specify the time elapsed. It was now half past the sixth hour, so the sections from one to six were completely lit and the seventh was illuminated halfway across which was fifty krometres. The amount of light increased in a counterclockwise direction as each krometre passed and the hour progressed. Raphyl had told him that their shift was from two until five, which was the average working day for most employees. He had said that he normally slept from seven until ten and therefore he reserved six and seven for his leisure time. Tom had explained to him that he was used to twenty-four hours being in a day and that hands went around the face twice to indicate this, to which Raphyl had laughed and commented on how complicated that system seemed. They took the lift to the twentieth floor where Tom saw that Kayleesh was waiting for them.

"You've got yourself a compsuit then?" she asked, her huge violet eyes twinkling.

"Hi Kayleesh. Yes. Do you like it?"

"You look great," she replied.

"What clothes do Augtopians wear then?" he asked, interested to know what she saw when she looked at him. She giggled, tossed back her golden hair, and leaned close to him. She whispered in his ear "We don't."

Tom felt himself blush but spoke quickly before embarrassment got the better of him. "*So,* what's the plan for this evening then?"

"We thought we'd take you to Six Seven – it's about the best place to go for mid-week entertainment. Strictly employees only," said Raphyl with a wink.

"Is it open from six until seven?" Tom ventured.

"He's learning," Raphyl said to Kayleesh. They all laughed. Tom was looking forward to experiencing a night out on Truxxe. He would normally go to a local pub once or twice a week at home. They walked along the passageway, the sound of some kind musical instrument and the murmur of conversation growing as they approached their destination. The music was loud now, although they could still speak over it. It reminded Tom of an amalgam of heavy rock and Celtic folk, which was confusing, but somehow enjoyable. The bar on the left-hand wall was a welcome sight. There were many ergonomic tables and chairs, filled with compsuit / hoody-wearing employees. Tom felt almost at home here. The lighting was subdued and there was a relaxed, friendly atmosphere, the sound of glasses chinking over the hubbub. If he closed his eyes, Tom could almost imagine he was in his local pub. They approached the bar.

"Hi son - a Truxxian and an Augtopian, yes?" said the Truxxian who was serving.

"That's right, Lan," Raphyl replied, leaning lazily on the bar. The barman filled two long glasses with liquid from two different containers mounted on optics. He placed the drinks on the bar. The glasses were conical and were supported on three legs so that they were elegant but stable looking. Raphyl took a sip from the thick, brown liquid in his glass. Kayleesh drank from her glass; a liquid which was so thin in consistency that she had to drink it in one sip almost before it could escape, like a gas. "And one for Tombo, please, Lan." Raphyl reached once more into his pocket for some Ds. Tom moved nearer to the bar and eyed the optics on the wall; Truxxian Gloop, Manfroidian Yets, Caloursish Ale, Augtopian Vapore, Spetulan Crander.

"I don't think you'll find what you're looking for on that shelf, son," laughed the barman. "Those drinks are on only on show because those are the main species we serve – saves me going out the back every few kroms to fill up the glasses. I don't think they'd suit your metabolism. Where are you from, son?"

"Earth."

"A human…" the barman raised his thick, purple monobrow. "Hmm… I'm not sure, I'll have a look out the back." He exited through a door behind him. Tom hadn't thought about alcohol since leaving Earth, with all the adjustments he had been mentally making to his new environment. But now that he was on the recreational floor, he felt a hankering for a cool pint. He licked his lips as he envisaged a cool, frothy pint of lager. For a moment he wondered whether there was yet another influential device in the bar which was emitting a silent pulse or something which made customers crave a drink. Then he cursed himself for being so paranoid, besides, if that were true then he was sure that the bar in his local pub had a similar device. Tom felt dismay as the barman returned a minute or so later empty-handed. But then he reached under the bar and produced a bowl, which he placed on the cluttered bar amongst the glasses, a few feet away from where Tom was standing.

"I can't see anything that's labelled up specifically for humans I'm afraid, son. So, I'll have to take a quick sample of your DNA so that I can find something best suited to you. Is that alright?"

"OK," Tom replied, a little confused.

"Just produce some saliva into the bowl and I'll go and get it tested," Lan said casually.

Tom looked around him apprehensively. He saw Kayleesh prompt him with a nod in the direction of the bowl on the bar. Tom turned towards it and shrugged. *I might as well make it a good one.* He proceeded to generate as much saliva in his mouth as he could and projected a ball of spittle into the dish. It flew four clear feet and landed dead centre in the base of the bowl. Tom smiled triumphantly. He looked at Raphyl and Kayleesh, at the barman. Were they disgusted? Why did they look like they'd just witnessed something amazing? Why was no one saying anything? It wasn't only his friends that were silent. He noticed that the general banter in Six Seven had succumbed to the hush. As he looked around, he felt like the stranger in an old western movie entering a saloon for the first time; even the music had stopped playing. All eyes were on him, mouths gaping open. Tom began to back away towards the door. Had he done something wrong? Had he unintentionally insulted them? Still no one said anything, until,

"Son!" exclaimed Lan, his lilac Truxxian mouth wide in a rapturous grin. Tom didn't say anything but ceased to back away. "Why didn't you tell us you were a Spotoon player?"

"A *what?*"

But before Lan could respond, Tom felt a hand on his shoulder. He turned around to face a muscular looking man with small, ratty eyes and leathery, burgundy skin. He looked as though he had spent too long in the gym and on a sun bed; although Tom supposed that perhaps his complexion was natural. He had four huge arms, two of which were supporting his burly body as his torso just seemed to taper to a point and ended a good foot off the ground. A benevolent smile betrayed his otherwise disquieting appearance. "Ghy Hasprin, Spotoon team captain. A range like that sure is a rarity," he said affably. He angled a protruding burgundy ear towards Tom, as though it were a greeting. Tom cautiously followed suit and tilted his head back at him.

"I'm Tom Bowler".

"You have a team?"

"Er,"

"For Spotoon?"

"Not exactly…" Tom began to explain that he just wanted a drink with his new colleagues, that didn't know what Spotoon was.

"Come and meet the guys!" Ghy interrupted and steered Tom away from the bar – much to his dismay – and towards a group at the opposite end of the room. Ghy looked like the most athletic of the group, whereas the rest of the bunch didn't have beer bellies exactly, but their posture and manner reminded Tom of his local's darts team who practiced on a Sunday afternoon. The Celtic rock folk music faded back in and the patrons proceeded to continue with their business. There were two Truxxians and Tom recognised Maytey Reeston, the express cuisine's cleaner and handy man. Maytey smiled at him.

"Hi Tom".

"You know Tom, Maytey?" Ghy sounded surprised.

"He's the new burger boy. Started today". Maytey's bright orange skin-tone looked muted in the subtle lighting of the venue. He was holding a conical glass in one of his long, sinewy arms.

"Why didn't you tell me that you'd met our new team member? I'm not letting this one go!" as if to confirm this, Ghy intensified the grip on his shoulder.

"I didn't know, Ghy," Maytey shrugged.

"Is it OK if I just get a drink?" Tom asked. He was a bit unsure of the situation and he felt the need to relax. It was all a bit overwhelming. He looked around for Raphyl and Kayleesh. They were talking at the bar. *Why didn't they come and rescue him?*

"Yes of course", Ghy smiled and then added, "After we've had a quick game". Tom's shoulders sank. "Maytey, set her up."

Maytey proceeded to pick up a dirty looking rag from a shelf on the adjoining wall and used it to wipe a disc, which hung above the shelf. The disc was approximately the size of a dinner plate. A circle with a diameter of roughly two centimetres had plainly been painted in the centre of the plate in green. Around that circle was a red ring about two centimetres wide and around that ring was an outer ring, which was of about the same thickness, painted orange. It looked like a peculiar parody of a small archery target. The team shuffled behind a line on the floor several paces away from the disc. *It is like darts.*

"We haven't got a match on tonight, but we often come here to practice. Why don't you go first, Tom?" Ghy released him from his clammy grip. Tom thought for a moment. He could guess the rules, but he didn't want to make himself look unnecessarily dim. He considered that if he massaged Ghy's sportsman's ego he might be able to delay his turn.

"You're the captain – why don't you go first?" Tom suggested, in what he hoped was a jovial manner.

"Quite right." Two muscular arms paced over to the chalked line, transporting Ghy's bulk. Tom watched tentatively as Ghy prepared himself. The beefy being cricked his wide neck, swallowed, punched one fist into the other, coughed and then focused on the target. Tom looked at the other team members, their collective gaze fixed on the disc. Just when Tom thought the captain wasn't going to do anything, a speeding wad of spittle soared out of Ghy's mouth and hit the heart of the target. He turned around and cocked an ear at Tom, a conceited expression on his face. Tom took this as his cue and stepped up to the chalk line. He felt slightly nauseated as Ghy's green saliva began to run slowly down the disc. He swallowed. He was conscious of several sets of eyes watching him. *What am I doing?* He ensued to produce as much saliva in his mouth as possible and prepared himself. He felt like he was fifteen again, lying on the motorway bridge with Nathan. They would each choose a colour or make of vehicle and aim to achieve the highest score. Nathan used to be able to time his so well that he could cause his spit to land on a motorcyclist's helmet. At first, Tom chose the easier options like buses and people-carriers, much to Nathan's amusement, but after one bored summer spent practising his technique, he was his friend's counterpart. Now he had to aim for an area not much bigger than a fifty-pence piece, two metres away. Tom jettisoned a pale-yellow mass from his mouth and watched it hurtle towards the target. It hit the left-hand side of the disc in the red ring. He was relieved that he hadn't made himself look foolish by not hitting the target at all. He was also pleased that he had not matched the captain's score. He knew from his father's experience that beating the boss or a new acquaintance - particularly one he was a bit scared of - would not win him good favour.

"Not bad, not bad." Ghy smiled his approval. The other team members inclined their ears at him. Perhaps this salutation was reserved to the team rather than a particular species. Tom responded politely. The three other members took their turns. One of the Truxxians got theirs just inside the green area, the other hit the orange ring and Maytey hit the red. Then Tom's ears registered those wonderfully Earthly-sounding words:

"Let me buy you a drink."

# CHAPTER 9

Tom opened a sleepy eye and focused on his new Truxxian watch. It took him several seconds to realise that it was ten krometres to one. He closed his eye again. He'd get up in a minute. His head hurt. The previous evening had gone better than he had expected. Lan had tested his DNA sample and matched it as closely as he could with the preferred beverage of the Glorbians - alcohol. Tom could have told him that he drank alcohol to begin with and wished he had done, but then he wouldn't have got onto the Spotoon team. He had played two more rounds with the team and had won one of them. Tom smiled as he remembered that he was especially delighted with this outcome because Kayleesh had ran up and hugged him. Her golden hair had smelled of cinnamon and felt like silk when he wrapped an arm around her. He was careful to observe how many drinks he owed because he was already indebted to Raphyl who had paid for his compsuit and timepiece when he had barely even known him. At least, he had *started* to take note of how many drinks he owed, but now he couldn't remember. He suspected that the concoction he had been drinking was stronger than his usual brew. It was so bright. His mouth felt dry. Tom couldn't believe that his spitting into a bowl was considered a great skill to possess here. He had never been gifted at any of the sports at school, yet he had been proficient at something considered as practically vandalism on Earth. Neither Raphyl nor Kayleesh were able to demonstrate more than a dribble into the bowl on the bar later that evening. At first Tom had thought that they were jesting him in order to make him feel like more of a victor, but it came to pass that they were being frank with him. Apparently, any spitting range at all for really was a rarity here. He chuckled at that notion.

*Paaaaaaaaaaaaaaarp!* It was the dreaded alarm. Tom sat up almost involuntarily. Why did he have to drink so much last night?

A yawning Raphyl greeted him in the staff room. He waved lethargically at Tom.

"Morning Raph," Tom yawned back. Jeffle and Jambole were also on the corner settee, deep in conversation. He was sure that the artificial daylight had been set to maximum, for the light was burning his retinas. Maytey Reeston came into the room. He looked as bad as Tom felt.

"Hey, fellow teammate," his voice was a little slurred. He rested an inebriated arm around Tom's shoulders." Everyone, meet our fifth teammate," he garbled.

"Maytey, are you still intoxicated?" an amused grin spread across Raphyl's fatigued face.

"Well…letsh just shay our celebrations went on until quite late this morning," Maytey slurred. He looked as though he was heading for the corner settee but walked into the wall instead. He halted, looked a little shocked and then began to snigger. His snigger grew into a loud guffaw. Jeffle and Jambole ceased their conversation. Maytey held his long orange arms in front of him, felt his way safely to the settee and plopped down. He looked across at Raphyl, one eye slightly squinting as though he was trying to focus. He jabbed a thumb in Tom's direction. "This one didn't make it to the after practish party though. He was all up for coming along," Maytey did an impression of a jogger's arm movements, "but then he fell ashleep in the lift, so we dropped him back to his apartment. Onesh we found it - ah that was a game and a half…" Maytey's eyes glazed over in apparent recollection. The door opened and Kayleesh entered, looking as bright and motivated as Tom had ever seen her.

"Whoa, you don't even look like you were out last night," Tom commented, realising that he must also still be a little drunk for his words to reflect his thoughts before he could stop them from tumbling out. Kayleesh smiled prettily.

"I have a complex morning beauty regime," she reasoned.

Tom felt his focus leave Kayleesh as his attention was suddenly engaged on the door as Miss Lolah entered. The wonderful Miss Lolah, with her beautiful, boxy bronze body and her perfectly circular camera lens eye. Tom was aware that these feelings weren't his own, but he was so drawn to her at this moment that nothing else mattered. Her voice this morning, however, had an edge to it.

"Maytey Reeston, Raphyl, Tom Bowler." All three stood up, abruptly. "According to my sensors, all three of you are over the intoxication limit. To avoid disciplinary action please take an abstemious pill from the first aid box before you begin your duties. Kayleesh, you have made a substantial effort to compose yourself so you will not be required to take one – I have faith that your skills will not be affected. The rest of you please take your posts." Tom still found her voice beautiful, despite today's sharp tone. The employees obeyed and Maytey and Raphyl fought their way to a cabinet on the wall. Miss Lolah lumbered through to her office without another word.

"I got them first!" Raphyl said, competitively.

"That's OK I don't want to sober up anyway," snarled Maytey as Miss Lolah's influence faded.

"No nor me really," agreed Raphyl, turning over a blister pack in his hand.

"What are they?" asked Tom.

"Abstemious pills – or party poopers as we call them. They sober you up without all that still being drunk at work feeling."

"Do they get rid of hangovers?" Tom asked hopefully. He began thinking how much he could sell these for on Earth. He would be a millionaire, even if Max was his only customer.

"Yes and no," Raphyl answered. "They *condense* your hangover. Rather than feeling rotten half of the day, they compress the feeling to two kroms of sheer awfulness, immediately after taking them. It's not a nice experience, but it does mean you get your head cleared for work and you don't feel lousy for hours like a natural hangover."

"Hmm." Tom considered this. He didn't like the idea of taking anything he was unsure of.

"We don't get a choice I'm afraid," said Raphyl, pushing a round, white tablet out of the packet and into Tom's hand. "Not if you work here."

Tom bit his lip. He watched Raphyl and Maytey each take a pill in their hands and then reluctantly put them in their mouths. Tom took a deep breath and followed suit. As soon as the tablet touched his tongue he crumpled to the floor. He felt as though his skull was being pulled down towards the ground by an invisible force. His jaw and his temples felt tight. His whole body was tense. He couldn't speak and he felt an incredible wave of nausea wash over him. His very nerve endings were twitching in a kind of spasmodic fit. His brain was filled with the unwanted emotions of guilt, paranoia and embarrassment. His head throbbed and his stomach lurched. He thought that he was going to be sick, but he couldn't get up. He couldn't move. Surely it wasn't supposed to go on for this long. Then just as soon as the experience had begun, he felt normal again. He was almost elated to be free from it. He stood up and saw that the others were also scrambling to their feet.

"Pretty rough, eh?" Maytey said.

"Wow. That was the most unpleasant, wonderful experience ever. I feel so much better now!"

"The room's stopped spinning anyway." Maytey put a hand to his head. They made their way through to the restaurant. Tom was amazed at how awake and refreshed he felt. He wasn't sure whether it was worth the period of nausea, pain and mental distress, but he was relieved to be able to function properly again. He watched Raphyl work as he had the previous day and talked to his colleagues between customers. He was continually amazed at the variety of species which consumed burgers and noted their strange and diverse customs. He felt that he was gaining more from the experience of observing the clientele than from the mundane business of taking food orders. He watched with curiosity as a huge, jelly-like creature devoured three burgers and a ruffleberry milkshake. The viscous being was semi-transparent so that the contents of its digestive system could be seen through its membrane. He was obviously not wearing a compsuit as he appeared to be naked; a large, translucent slug masticating a stodgy meal which could be seen churning around inside it. Tom was glad that he had taken an abstemious pill, as he was sure he would have certainly been sick otherwise.

"Hey, you must have picked it up by now. You said yourself it looked easily – why don't you serve the next customer?" Raphyl leaned back against the shelving and gestured a hand in the direction of the till.

"Yeah OK," Tom said confidently. He took his place at the till and familiarised himself with the controls. *Touch screen, green button. Simple.*

"I'm just going to the sanitation room – back in a krom", said Raphyl and walked in the direction of the staff room.

A customer approached the counter. It was a species Tom had not seen before. The being was wearing a compsuit because it appeared to be wearing jeans and a dark brown hooded top with The Foo Fighters written across it. From underneath the hood protruded a long, pallid, beak-like appendage. Its eyes were small, and a flesh-coloured claw held out a fistful of Ds. The long beak opened. Tom leaned forwards slightly and looked attentively at him, ready to take his order. He was horrified, however, when, instead of normal speech, Tom heard an ear-splitting squawk. Who was this? Why couldn't he understand him? He wanted to cover his hands over his ears to mute the sound, but he felt that it would be rude to do so - he didn't want to offend him. The creature leaned closer and opened its mouth wider and a second, louder squawk was released.

"I... I don't know what you're saying," Tom spluttered. The being looked stunned and confused and took a few steps back. It squawked again. Why wasn't Raphyl around when he needed him?

"Jambole!" Tom called to the chef who was placing an order for Kayleesh on the shelving unit behind him. Jambole looked at him through the shelving slats. Tom could detect a look of uncertainty in the scaly-faced man's obtruding yellow eyes. He saw his mouth open to speak but all that came out was a discord of sounds, hisses and whines. What was happening? Where was Raphyl? His heart thumping, he turned to Kayleesh's counter, but she was running across the restaurant, past the customers, past the seating area. Where was she going? What was she running from? What was happening? He looked around, his heart in his throat. He was aware of a rising commotion and a cacophony of noise as panic-stricken visitors rose from their tables and approached the counter. He could hear a mixture of diverse sounds, each growing in intensity as they reached him. Some were discharging a painfully low hum, which he could sense in his stomach. Others were releasing high-pitched ticks or rambling gabble. He was sure that some sounds were being transmitted directly in his head, but he couldn't decipher what they were or where they were coming from. In terror he left Raphyl's till and fled across the restaurant.

"Kayleesh! Wait for me!"

# CHAPTER 10

Tom kept running. Where could Kayleesh be going? Did she know what was happening? He kept her wave of blonde hair in view as he pushed through dozens of people, breathing hard as he ran, the dissonance of panicked alarm, from all the visitors, ringing in his ears. He looked out for signposts for some kind of clue, but to his horror, he could no longer read them. Instead of words indicating the direction of various facilities in the station, strange symbols were in their place. The directional arrows themselves were even a different shape, so Tom had no way of understanding them. Was he dreaming? He picked up his pace as he saw Kayleesh's golden mane flit behind a group of people and through a door at the end of a busy passageway. He dived through a mass of visitors who were blocking his path and reached the door. He entered a small, white room. Kayleesh was in there with five other breathless employees who had evidently also just arrived. Tom could not read their expressions.

"Kayleesh?" Tom asked, but she just looked at him. He noticed that one of them, an older Truxxian, was opening a transparent cabinet on the far wall with a silver key. Inside the cabinet was a red, octagonal button. The Truxxian pressed it with his elongated lilac fingers, closed the cabinet calmly and removed the silver key. He turned to the group.

"Right – the situation is now back under control. Thank you everyone," he said in tranquil tones and swiftly left the room. The other employees filed out calmly after him. Tom grabbed Kayleesh by the arm.

"What was all that about?"

"The ALSID went offline. Happens quite often. Don't worry it's all right now – as you can probably tell."

"Sorry, *what?* The *ALSID?*" Tom kept up with her pace as she efficiently retraced her steps, through a much calmer station.

"The Atmospheric Linguistic Spectrum Interpretation Device system – the unit which controls the translation field."

"Right…" Tom was beginning to catch on. "Is that why I couldn't understand anything that anyone was saying? Because the atmospheric linguistic thingy wasn't working?" Kayleesh nodded. "And that's why none of the signs made any sense because the system translates not only speech but written language?" he said, excitedly.

"Not only that, but it translates other types of communication such as electromagnetic, motion, psychic conversations. It covers the whole conversational spectrum – hence the name. Pretty clever, when you think about it, I suppose. The system has a device in each sector of the station. You can see one up there, look." She pointed up to the high ceiling where Tom could make out what looked like a large, silver sprinkler-head.

"Right...and that button that that guy just pushed was the central control?"

"Correct. That was the ALSID control room for the whole system. There are six employees – each from a different department – who have been entrusted with a key to reset the unit should it malfunction. That's why we all congregated in the control room. And that *guy* was Hansk, the head of fuel supplies."

"And you've been entrusted with one of the keys?"

"That's right." She had the air of slight smugness, although her sweet, friendly nature didn't make her unapproachable.

"You weren't a head prefect at school were you?"

"A what?"
"Never mind."

When they arrived back at the restaurant, Kayleesh coolly took her position and began serving the first in a long line of customers. Raphyl was serving the beaked creature whom Tom hadn't understood and had run away from. Tom felt embarrassed about his startled behaviour and stood behind Raphyl, with his head bowed.

"Where did you go? I only left you for a krom." Raphyl handed the customer a tray of food and smiled half-heartedly at the next person in line.

"You picked a great time to disappear," Tom said, sarcastically. "I followed Kayleesh – I didn't know what was happening. No one warned me about the ALSID system."

"It's no big deal - happens all the time," Raphyl grinned at him as he pressed the green confirm button on the till.

"So I heard." Tom mumbled.

"Want to serve the next customer? Or are you going to run away screaming again?" Raphyl laughed.

"OK." They switched places and he added "And I wasn't screaming."

Tom served the next five customers without any further difficulties, quite enjoying being occupied rather than simply watching Raphyl.

"Tom," Jambole Farr called through the shelving. "I need a hand with these crates. Have you got a krom?"

"Yeah, sure." Tom replied and wandered around the back of the shelving and into the kitchen area to meet him. He had not been in this area of the restaurant before. He could see two long stainless-steel work surfaces, a large freestanding washing-up bowl full of water in which some kind of hand-held appliance was soaking and various cooking equipment. Jephle looked as though he was preparing salad, although Tom didn't recognise any of the vegetables he was slicing. Jambole was wiping his soapy hands on a large piece of cloth.

"Right, the restaurant backs onto a cargo bay where the deliveries are shipped in. We've got six crates of burgers, a tank of carbonated fruit water and four cartons of ruffleberries to collect. Jephle? Want to give us a hand too? The flansnips can wait."

Jephle placed his knife down on his chopping board and joined them. He looked up at Tom sheepishly, from his terminally cowered stance "Enjoying the new job then?" he said in hushed tones.

"Yes thanks. I'm getting the hang of it," he replied. Jephle's eyes remained on him, although he did not say anything more. Something about the way he was looking at him made Tom feel ill at ease. Perhaps he was waiting for Tom to elaborate, but thankfully the discomfiture Tom felt was broken by Jambole.

"Come on then you two, there are customers waiting." Jambole, opened a heavy-looking double door and waked through. Tom keenly followed, with Jephle shuffling behind him. The door opened out into a vast freight bay, which was vibrant with distribution ships delivering various consignments. Tom could see a ship to his far left, from which several employees and delivery people were carrying large green boxes. To his right, some kind of hovering forklift truck was manoeuvring gigantic crates from another ship. The area was immense, although nothing as large as the docking bay, Tom noticed. The craft which had docked behind the restaurant had its name splashed above an access ramp in bright yellow; The Cluock. There was a figure standing at the top of the ramp, standing next to some crates; a short, grey being, perhaps only half the height of Tom. The creature made his way slowly down the ramp on two stout, hairy, bare feet. Tom got the impression that he was quite elderly. He was wearing a dirty brown sash across his plump body and Tom could detect a distinct odour as he neared them. Jambole walked off and presently returned driving one of the hovering forklift trucks. Tom wished that he could drive one as Jambole ascended the ramp with ease. He followed Jephle up the ramp and helped him carry the cartons of ruffleberries while Jambole had the evidently pleasurable task of carting the crates of meat to the restaurant kitchen. There was a storage area just inside the kitchen, which the truck could just about squeeze inside to unload the goods. Tom stood and watched Jambole lower the third crate onto the storage room floor with fascination.

"Can I have a go, Jambole?"

"Maybe another time Tom – these things are a lot harder to control than they look. Took me months to perfect the technique." He replied, much to Tom's annoyance. Then he whooshed out of the room and back up the incline. Tom sighed, crestfallen, and went to help Jephle roll the tank of fruit water down the ramp. Once everything had been safely stored away, the deliveryman offered Jambole an electronic device into which he proceeded to key in some sort of confirmation code.

"Would you like to order the next batch today?" The grey-skinned man asked Jambole, optimistically.

"Today? That's a little soon isn't it? I don't know how long this batch will last us yet. No… we'll contact you when we need more supplies as usual."

"Very well." The man forced a smile although his eyes betrayed thinly disguised disappointment. "We'll wait until we hear from you then." The stumpy being took back the device and walked back up the ramp without another word.

"I'd like to apply for a job."

"OK and what is your name sir?"

"Hannond Putt."

"OK Mr. Putt. If you'd like to move along to desk number four and speak to the attendant, she will be able to arrange for the relevant scan." The Truxxian behind desk number one smiled at him and proceeded to serve the next person in line. Grumpily, Hannond shuffled across the busy reception area, past two more snaking queues and reluctantly waited at the end of what was seemingly the longest line of all. Glorbians are even more renowned for their lack of patience than their lack of hygiene.

"Are you coming along to play Spotoon tonight, Tom?" Maytey Reeston asked as he swept around the counter area. Tom watched the motions of the broom with silent fascination as it apparently ingested any debris within a metre radius. It automatically collected and stacked any fallen coins in a separate transparent tube at the side.

"Well I was planning on a quiet night after last night - I was pretty hung over this morning. Plus, I still haven't got any money until I get paid."

"That's not a Spotoon player's way of thinking!" Maytey glared at him. His huge orange face cracked into the huge grimace that Tom had learned to have been a smile. "No, we're not having a big night out or anything – we're just planning on having a game or two round Ghy's if you're up for it. He has his own board." Tom didn't like to decline his offer and he didn't see the harm in going to Ghy's apartment for a while, particularly if it involved not spending any money - money that he didn't have. He decided that it might be quite fun and nodded.

"Yes, I'll be there. Where does he live?"

"I'd like to arrange for an employment scan please." Hannond said as politely as possible. His flat, stubby feet were aching him after standing in queues for several hours. Although, he was certain that it would be his ears that would be aching more by the time he finally met up again with Schlomm - he may have been able to predict his brother's temper but was still unable to escape it.

"What kind of position are you looking for, sir?" Came the whine of the desk attendant. An olive-green face peered at him over the desk; a listless expression was spread across her three eyes. Each eye blinked slowly at him in turn.

"I want to work in the TSS sewage works if there are any jobs going," Hannond said, hopefully.

"Sir, there are *always* vacancies in the sewage works," she said. She hovered her ergonomic desk chair across to a filing cabinet behind her. She opened one of the drawers, flicked through various documents and files and took out a stack of paper. She glided back to the desk, where Hannond was waiting, rubbing one of his aching feet with his hands. He stood up as straight as he could and took the wad of paper from her outstretched hand.

"Fill in these details then please return the completed form to the attendant behind desk five and we will begin to process your application," the attendant said in her whiny tone.

"Form? It's more like half a huxleberry tree!" complained Hannond.

# CHAPTER 11

Tom had finished his shift, filled himself up on a meal from the restaurant and gone back to his lodgings to wash and change into his compsuit. He was on his way to Ghy's apartment. He was looking forward to having some money so that he could live on more than just the meals that were provided free with his job; he was looking forward to trying something different to eat. He knew that his parents would not be very pleased if they knew he was surviving each day on a burger and various side orders from a fast food restaurant. He hadn't had a lot of time to think about his parents, he had been so busy becoming accustomed to his new life and learning the local decorum. But he did miss them. He had spent eighteen years living under their roof and had always been close to them. He was just feeling the tinges of homesickness when a door along the passageway opened and a large, orange head poked out.

"Tom! Come on, Ghy's just setting up." Maytey called cheerfully. Ghy's apartment was markedly larger than his own. The walls were decorated the same pale blue as Tom's apartment. One side of the large main room had the same basic layout: bed, storage cupboard, kitchen area, dining area. The other side, however, was evidently dedicated to entertainment. There was a free-standing bar, some kind of table game that Tom did not recognise, a comfortable-looking seating area and, of course, a Spotoon board. Ghy's lodgings were comparably more superior than Tom's. Perhaps he held a more senior position in the company or was more established at TSS. The team inclined their ears at Tom as he entered. He returned the greeting.

"Impressive," Tom whistled in admiration as he looked round the room.

"It's not a bad apartment is it?" Ghy gave Tom his largest grimace. "Drink?"

Tom nodded "Why not?"

"I have a bottle of an alcoholic beverage somewhere," he said, picking up various bottles on the bar and reading the labels. "Ah – Glorbian's finest." Ghy unscrewed the cap of what looked like a bottle of whisky and poured some of the contents into a glass. The glass was not unlike the conical, tripod-based glasses Tom had drunk from at Six Seven the previous night. He handed the drink to Tom. Tom was aware of the other team members watching him as he took a sip. He coughed at the inebriating taste of the drink, much to the amusement of the other guests. He raised the glass slightly and smiled genuinely. The aftertaste was pleasing.

"Not bad." Tom took another sip and set the glass down on the bar next to the others.

"Ransel – why don't you start?" Ghy took a gulp from a glass of bright green gassy-looking liquid and pointed at one of the portly Truxxian players. Ransel willingly took his place behind a line which had been etched into the floor. He puffed out his over-sized Spotoon-player's stomach, intertwined his long, Truxxian fingers, palms outward, and pushed his arms out in front of him in a stretch, readying himself. He took two, noisy breaths and then shot out a ball of spittle at the board. A grey blob landed in the red middle zone. He made a gesture similar to a shrug, which suggested that he wasn't overly pleased with his score and returned to the bar. Tom went next, at Ghy's signal, and managed to hit the green centre circle. He grinned as the others cheered. The other Truxxian, Chazner also managed to strike the green circle. Tom cheered with his teammates. Maytey and Ghy both managed to get within the red ring. After the round, Ghy walked across the room on two of his muscular, maroon arms. Tom thought that it was a pity that Ghy couldn't make use of his Herculean frame in the sport he played; it seemed like such a waste to just be playing a pub game like Spotoon. The Truxxians were tall for their breed and heavy-looking, although Tom doubted that they would have the strength that Ghy undoubtedly possessed. Maytey didn't look very powerful to Tom, with his fragile-looking limbs; the scariest thing about Maytey was his smile. Tom guessed that this motley crew of characters in the team might have appeared amusing to an outsider. Even more so now that he had joined them; a tall but slender human who had blundered his way through physical education at school and had never lifted a dumbbell in his life. Tom had never felt the camaraderie of being in a team. He was beginning to enjoy the fellowship and the feeling of belonging to a large group, having been used to such a small group of friends back home. He felt a pang of guilt – Nathan and his cousin were exceptional friends to have and he hadn't been a great friend to them by leaving them so suddenly. He wished that they were with him; that they could join him in his experiences here on Truxxe.

"Hey, Tom," Ransel broke his thoughts "another game?"

Hannond flicked through the thick scan application form, checking that he had filled every section; he did not want to have to complete it all over again. He shook his writing hand in an attempt to loosen the joints a little; it was aching from writing for so long. Schlomm hadn't mentioned anything about a form to him. He had said that getting a job on Truxxe – particularly in TSS – was "easier than falling down a Glorbian pit." And there were a lot of pits on Glorb. Once he was confident that the application form was completed, he loathingly took a place at the end of the line in front of desk number five. He groaned at the size of the queue, and as he did so, inadvertently let a ripple of flatulence erupt from his bottom. He looked around him, hoping that no one would notice. People had noticed, however, and were quite vocal about it as half of the beings in the queue were forced to leave, holding their various noses and complaining in disgust. Hannond stepped forward a dozen places in the queue, grinning to himself. Why hadn't he thought of this before?

Ghy poured his team-mates another round of drinks from various containers from his well-stocked bar. They were halfway through their third game of Spotoon when Tom, being closest to the door, heard someone knocking. The others didn't seem to hear as they were cheering rowdily at Maytey's green circle hit. The knocking came again, this time an impatient thumping. This time everyone turned round.

"Expecting anyone else, Ghy?" Chazner asked, sipping his Truxxian Gloop.

"No," Ghy said slowly. He pulled himself up straight on his heavy arms, shoulders square and defiant. He walked over to the door, slowly, almost cautiously. Tom could sense nervousness in his manner, despite his apparently confident gait. A flurry of thumping recurred, louder this time. Then shouts:

"Hasprin?" Boomed a gruff voice. "Hasprin? You and your pathetic pack of teammates in there?"

Tom tightened his grip on his glass in fear. The room was silent. The pause before Ghy spoke seemed infinite.

"What do you want, Bulken?"

"Just a friendly chat, Hasprin," came the reply, although his tone suggested otherwise. Tom heard muffled laughter. This Bulken character was evidently not alone.

"It's late, Bulken, why don't you and your sorry band of dribblers go back to your own floor?" Ghy retorted, rather bravely Tom thought.

"Past your bedtime is it, Hasprin?" the deep voice roared with laughter.

"Grow up, Bulken."

"Are you and your little friends practising for the Big Match?" the voice mocked, ominously. Big Match? Tom hadn't been told anything about a big match. Was this Bulken something to do with Spotoon? He gulped and edged slowly away from the door towards the safety of his teammates. He was glad that he had made this move when Ghy, apparently having been pushed too far, suddenly threw the door open. A colossal creature filled the doorway, all biceps and pectorals. His face was almost one big, green scowl. Yellow saliva hung from a matted clump of brown facial hair. Bulken entered the room, anger encircling his physique like a rip current. The stench of his raspy breath made Tom feel nauseated. Four other beings trailed in after him, each a different species, although all taller and better built than Tom. One of them laid his eyes on Tom and hissed,

"There's the new boy, Baff." Baff Bulken turned to face Tom and his grin widened. He walked purposefully towards him and pressed his face against Tom's. Tom felt nauseated as a sliver of thick, yellow saliva was pressed from Baff's face and onto his own. The stench of his warm breath made his stomach lurch. A mighty, green hand gripped Tom coolly around the neck.

"Take your hands off him, Bulken," Ghy warned, coming up behind him. To Tom's relief, Baff released his grip and turned to Ghy.

"I was only inspecting your... fresh blood," he said menacingly. "I must say though, Ghy, it was very resourceful of you to have picked a human - you *do* know your sport."

"Better than *you* do." Ghy stood close to his rival, faces almost touching. Tom rubbed his neck. He didn't want to be here, but what else could he do?

"Let's just hope that his fate doesn't follow that of your last fifth member!" Baff said, forebodingly.

"I think it's time you left, Bulken." Maytey said and stepped forward, guarding Tom from Baff's reach. Baff laughed "And you're going to stop me are you, Reeston? What are you going to do, orange-skin? *Dazzle* me to death?" he held up a hand as if shielding his eyes from a bright light and laughed. From his obstructed view over Maytey's shoulder, Tom saw the expression on Ghy's face change. His irritated, slightly nervous countenance detonated into one of pure rage. He thumped his right fist into his left palm.

"Ooh have I found the trigger, Hasprin? Have I gone too far?" Baff mocked.

"Oh yes, Bulken - way too far. I didn't want any trouble tonight, but you haven't given me a choice I'm afraid."

Tom stood, helpless, unguarded. Maytey, Chazner and Ransel stood tall and stepped into the centre of the room. Baff's team members followed suit and squared up to them. Tom could see it coming; he had been in similar situations before. Usually Tom would be hiding under a pub table by now but there weren't any tables nearby. He looked around, frantically, before diving behind the bar. He was being a coward, he knew, but he didn't owe these people anything. Fresh blood? What *had* happened to the team member he had seemingly replaced? He hadn't been told about rival teams or 'Big Matches'. What had he got himself into? He closed his eyes and cowered, hands on top of his head, and waited. He heard a thump. Who had thrown the first punch? He daren't look. The thump was followed by another, which was quickly proceeded by a succession of punches and thuds. The next few minutes were some of the strangest Tom had experienced on Truxxe. The sound of nine creatures battling and brawling on the hard apartment floor was horrifically terrifying. Not only could he hear the sound of fist against flesh, or appendage against appendage, the sounds which some of the beings themselves were creating caused Tom the most alarm. Despite the ALSID system translating their various languages, the noise of threatening hisses, snarls and cries of agony conjured up the worst images in Tom's mind. Who was making what noise? Who was winning? Perhaps he should be brave and help out his team-mates? Before he could decide, he felt something heavy fall on him and he blacked out.

Tom opened his eyes. His head hurt. Where was he? Wherever he was, the room he was in was intensely lit. Once his eyes had become accustomed to the light a figure came into his vision. At first sight, Tom thought that they must be very tall, until he realised that he was lying in a bed and that the figure was standing over him.

"Where am I?" Tom croaked.

"Floor seventeen; the clinicarium," came the gentle reply.

"Clinicarium?" Tom croaked, his head feeling as though it was full of dough.

"That's right – hospital floor." Tom tried to focus on who was speaking. He saw that it was a smooth-skinned oceanic-looking creature. He assessed by her tone that she was female. He tried not to flinch as he spotted six distinctive tentacles floating about her body out of a blue and white TSS robe, each one holding a terrifying looking instrument. He instinctively pulled the crisp white sheet up around his neck.

"What's happening?"

"It seems you're going to need some re-constructive surgery Tom... Bowler," she read his name from a device held in one of her addendum arms.

"Re-constructive surgery? What do you mean?"

"It was quite a fight – you were very brave, Tom. In fact, I'm surprised you haven't been shouting out for more pain killers... with injuries like yours." She lowered her head, ruefully.

With injuries like his? What had happened? What did she mean? Tom tried to move his legs. He moved his arms again for reassurance, wiggled his fingers and toes. His extremities all seemed to be present and correct. He opened his mouth to protest, but the nurse silenced him with a cool, clammy blue tentacle on his lips. "Ssh, now, get some rest. Brave, brave boy." The nurse turned to leave when he heard a familiar voice.

"Medic Flonce." It was Raphyl. The indolent Truxxian approached the bed. Tom smiled weakly.

"I'm not sure you should be in here, young man. Your friend is in a very bad way," she said sternly.

"Who, Tombo? From what I hear he wasn't even in the fight." Tom saw his face crease. "He spent the whole time cowering behind the bar." He let out a chortle of laughter.

"Then how do you explain his injuries?" Medic Flonce challenged him, crossing two of her tentacles across her large chest.

"What injuries? Looks alright to me – looks like the same strange pink human he was before," he grinned at the two of them. The medic's face fell.

"Human?"

"Er, yes," said Tom, quietly.

"Oh!" She threw her tentacles in the air in disbelief. "I thought you were a… oh never mind. In that case there's nothing wrong with you, you're perfectly fine. Up you get then, we need the bed for someone who actually needs it!" Her change of tone was dramatic.

Stunned, Tom pulled off the bedclothes and stood up. He didn't feel perfectly fine.

"But my head… I don't feel right," he protested.

"All your limbs are intact, everything else is in check. It's only a headache, you'll be fine, boy."

Bewildered, Tom moved away from the bed and followed Raphyl out of the ward. Raphyl was still laughing.

"I'm glad you're so amused by it all," Tom snarled. "First I wake up in a hospital bed with a pounding headache with no idea how I got there and then I get kicked off the ward by a psychotic octopus!"

"I'm laughing because it's the second morning in a row that you've suffered because of drink".

"What do you mean? This is not a hangover Raphyl, I only had two glasses," Tom said crossly at Raphyl's trivial remark.

"Yes, but this time your head hurts because the bar fell on you," Raphyl grinned at him. Tom couldn't stay mad at his friend and joined in. "It actually fell on your head!" He burst into laughter. Tom scowled at him.

"Hey, do those abstemious pills work for anything?"

"I'm afraid not – then we wouldn't need the clinicarium."

"Good point."

"You'll be all right. Hey, let's go and see the rest of your teammates – they're in the next ward along." Tom halted. He wasn't sure how he felt about Ghy and the others anymore. After all, there were details they hadn't informed him about; like how dangerous a sport Spotoon actually was.

"Aren't we supposed to be at work?"

"Work? You're granted a day off if you wake up in hospital, Tom." Raphyl slapped him warmly on the back.

"And what about you?"

"Well... you need someone to look after you, don't you?" he grinned. "Don't worry, Kayleesh can manage – she's got one of the twilighter's helping her out." Tom got the feeling that Raphyl was enjoying his excuse not to work, but he was glad to see a friendly face. The two of them walked along a pristine, white corridor and through an archway along one of the walls, which led into another ward. There were six beds in the room, the first three of which were occupied by Ransel, Maytey and Ghy. Chazner was standing next to Maytey's bed talking to him. "It was Chazner that informed Miss Lolah about the incident," Raphyl enlightened him. Chazner looked a little shaken, as they approached him, but otherwise unharmed. Tom looked down at Maytey. He was stunned to see that his head was a uniform pale pink, a sorrowful expression on his swollen face.

"What happened to you?" Tom asked, quietly.

"I'm just badly bruised, Tom." Maytey forced a brave smile, although his eyes were filled with milky, white moisture. He tried to sit himself up, but Tom could see that he was wincing as he did so.

"Don't move, Maytey. Just rest," a Truxxian medic called as she walked past him with a pile of bandages. Maytey obeyed and let himself sink back down into the bed in a huge sigh.

"Tom Bowler." Tom recognised Ghy's voice. He and Raphyl turned to the bed behind them. Tom still felt a little awkward for not supporting them in their fight, despite the circumstances. But his embarrassment was soon quashed.

"How's our star player?" Ghy smiled up at him.

"I'm... fine. Bit shaken, you know," he replied, gallantly.

"Ah, well done for sticking around, lad. Done us proud you did." Tom didn't know how to respond to that, so he decided not to. "Hey, Tom. You should see the BBs!"

"The..." Tom began, confused.

"Baff Bulken's team," Raphyl finished. "I had a peak at them on the way down... all five of them are lying there groaning in the ward – bunch of dribblers."

"Why do you call them dribblers?"

"It's a Spotoon insult. They can't produce more than a dribble," Ghy told him.

"Ah, right. Makes sense," Tom nodded. "So, what happened? Are you badly hurt?"

"Me? Tom, I've been in worse confrontations than that. I'll be out of here today. Can't stand clinicarium food!" Tom could see that Ghy was making light of it though as his breathing was shallow and his smile, strained.

"And the others?" Tom looked around him at the other occupied beds.

"Ransel's sprained a foot, but Maytey will be back sweeping floors in a couple of rotations. Nothing serious. As I said, you should see the BBs!"

"Hmm… I'd rather not," Tom admitted.

"It took you *all night* to apply for a pathetic job as a cess pool boy?" Schlomm glared at his brother as he ascended the Cluock's entry ramp.

"These things take time," Hannond shrugged. "You wouldn't believe the rigmarole… anyway I won't bore you with the details. The main thing is, I got the job."

"Perfect!" Schlomm rubbed his grubby, rough hands together. "When do you start?"

"In two rotations time."

"Perfect — by then the meat consignment should be in circulation and the Glorbian crystals should be germinating nicely in the bellies of the unsuspecting punters." He grinned a wide, malicious grin. "And then, my brother, it's harvest time!"

# CHAPTER 12

Tom Bowler decided that he wanted a quiet afternoon. Raphyl had explained to him that the period after the third hour and before the sixth was actually known as "post midsun". Despite the fact that Truxxe did not orbit a sun. Tom still hadn't fully recovered from his ordeal and he didn't want to risk inducing any more trouble for a while, or at all if he could help it. He just wanted to stay out of the path of any potential danger and hide away in his apartment for the rest of the rotation. Raphyl, however, had other ideas.

"What's the point in staying in your room? The BBs are all in the clinicarium and you've got a whole post midsun to enjoy – we've got a free day off, Tom!"

"So you keep saying," Tom held his hand to his pounding head. Raphyl did have a point, he knew. None of them could hurt him if they were all in the confines of a hospital ward. He thought for a moment. "Did you know the BBs were dangerous?"

Raphyl stifled a laugh. "They're renowned rivals to Hasprin's Legion, Tom. Didn't Ghy tell you about them?"

"No. No he didn't. In fact, I didn't even know *our* team had a name."

"Really? You're quite new to all this then?"

"You *could* say that." Tom was feeling rather overwhelmed.

"And, of course, there's the Gharka. They're another team – cess pool boys, mostly."

"They sound charming," said Tom sarcastically. "Just how many teams are there?"

"Hundreds I should think, on Truxxe alone. In TSS? About a dozen. Some are serious players; some are just low-leaguers – they play just for fun."

"And Hasprin's Legion?"

"Oh, they're serious players," Raphyl grinned.

"That's what I feared."

"I bet you haven't been off the station yet, have you?" Raphyl didn't wait for a reply. "There's more to Truxxe than TSS – let's go outside." Raphyl picked up his slow pace to a steady amble.

*So much for a restful day in my room, I'm going to step out into an alien atmosphere instead.* The two of them descended to the swarming foyer and Tom followed Raphyl in the direction of the docking area. They turned before they reached the port and walked on through another high-walled bustling reception area. Tom was amazed at the number of desks which lined the walls, each boasting winding queues of customers in various attire.

"Looks like there are a lot of enquiries – look at all the people," Tom pointed out.

"TSS is a big place. It's always like this here. We'll have to join a queue ourselves in a krom. Don't worry, we won't have to wait too long." Tom was glad about that – some of the queuing customers looked rather fatigued. They reached a grand-looking resplendent double door at the far end of the room. Raphyl pushed a circular button on the wall and the doors hummed open. Tom hesitated.

"Don't worry," Raphyl reassured him. "You'll be able to breathe out here, if you don't need breathing apparatus in there. It's the same. Air's the same, gravity's the same – everything. Oh, except for there's no artificial lighting. And no ALSID."

"So, how do we see and how are we going to be able to understand each other?"

"That's why we need to queue."

A surge of excitement began to grow in Tom's stomach. It was easy to forget that he was on alien soil when inside the service station, it was so Earthly in many respects. Tom's headache was subsiding, and his spirit of adventure was alive once more.

As they stepped outside, he looked around him in awe. Raphyl was right. The utter blackness was in stark contrast to the bright luminescence of the interior. He strained to see anything, but his eyes had not yet adjusted and for all he knew, they could be standing inside a cupboard.

Tom eventually detected a shape in his peripheral vision. There was a Truxxian standing to his left with his back to him. He realised that he was looking at yet another queue. Tom joined Raphyl at the end of it. A short while later they reached the front of the queue and were faced with another line, a row of stumpy metallic boxes. The boxes were stacked in twos; one cube on top of another.

"Could we rent one for three hours, please?" Raphyl said in his usual indolent tone. He handed a credit-card sized badge to an attendant. The employee was an Augtopian male, the same species as Kayleesh. Tom subtly covered his private area with his hands, despite his compsuit. He hadn't forgotten what Kayleesh had said about her race not wearing clothes. The Augtopian took the badge and knelt by one of the stacked duos of metallic boxes. He inserted it into a slot on its flat top. Tom jumped as the boxes whirred into life. They lifted several inches off the floor, as one, on a cushion of air. The upper cube spun round, and Tom could make out a grilled speaker; it was a robot. It reminded Tom of an even cruder, much shorter version of Miss Lolah. Thankfully, this robot didn't have the same effect on him as the pherobot. He found it difficult not to laugh as he looked at the comical looking, squat little mechanical creature. It appeared to be reading the card as it generated the kind of sounds his computer made when it read a disc. Then it spoke in a surprisingly deep, masculine voice.

"Card valid. Language one – Truxxe, Ranlandian. Please specify language two." Raphyl looked at Tom.

"Your language needs to be inputted next, human." Raphyl grinned. "Where are you from?"

"Earth".

"Is there only one language on Earth?" Raphyl looked confused.

"Oh… England. I speak English," said Tom.

"Language two – Earth, English," the Augtopian said to the robot. The robot made another series of noises as it processed the information.

"Language two confirmed." The Augtopian handed Raphyl what looked to Tom like the end of a lead.

"Thank you. I'm just showing Tom, here, the sights."

"Enjoy your tour, Tom," the attendant smiled at him. Tom realised that by keeping his hands crossed he was actually drawing attention *to* rather than *from* the region he was trying to conceal, so he turned away at his first opportunity. He blushed awkwardly, wishing that Kayleesh hadn't given him that information. They walked away from the desk and into the blackness.

"So, why do we need the pet robot?" Tom whispered.

"It's a portable ALSID. It translates for us while we're out of the territory of the interior ALSID units," Raphyl explained.

"So why doesn't everyone just carry one of these around the station?"

"Are you joking? Believe me, after leading this bulky bot round for a few hours you'd see its limitations. Besides… it's probably a thousand times smaller than the station's ALSID system – it's not nearly as powerful and has a short range. It's not just a communication device though." Raphyl looked down at the box shape, hovering patiently at his feet.

"Light on," he commanded. Instantly, the robot was the centre of a pool of pale-yellow light. He turned to Tom. "Now we can see where we're going. Handy." Now that he could see the robot in more detail, Tom saw that the purple TSS logo was inscribed in the left-hand corner of the top face of the machine. Next to it was a symbol in red of a pickaxe and an octagonal button was indented into the metalwork. In the right-hand corner was stamped the words: *ALSID Light Bot no. 379*.

"I didn't bring you out here to admire the robots, Tom. Come on, there's a place I know you might like to visit." Raphyl tugged at the lead and the robot followed behind him gracefully, its head-cube twisting a full circle before facing the direction in which it was travelling.

"Why does it have to have a lead?" asked Tom.

"So that it can follow. It hasn't got a lens; you might have noticed. It's basically blind."

"Oh," Tom almost felt himself pity the machine. "Why's that then?"

"Probably too costly to make them too sophisticated. You don't want too many employees running around out here with expensive equipment." Tom nodded at Raphyl's half-logic and looked around as they ventured away from the station. The vastness and stillness of the flat land across which they were walking was the antithesis of the bustling, energetic nucleus of the service station. He could hear the indistinct chatter fade and the glow which radiated from the tremendous construction diminished with each step. Tom was almost fooled into believing that it was night-time again, even though he had only been awake for three Truxxian hours. He looked up. The star configurations were unfamiliar from his standpoint on this alien world. He thought he could see the kaleidoscopic gleam of a nebula if he squinted. He wondered how far he was from home. Was one of those pinpoints of light his sun? Was one of them even the Milky Way?

He felt his toe hit something hard. The suddenness of the pain broke his thoughts. He looked down to see what the offending obstacle was and saw the robot hovering in front of him.

"Please be careful," the robot admonished him, before proceeding its path in Raphyl's wake. Raphyl laughed without turning around, he had obviously guessed what had happened.

"It's not funny. That hurt," complained Tom. He could imagine the frivolous grin on Raphyl's amused face. He hobbled up to him – partly to catch up and partly to avoid the mishap recurring. "So, where are we going?"

"Well, as you're still pretty new to Truxxe I've thought of the perfect place to take you. It's got the whole tourist thing going on, so you can learn more about our planet - if that's what you really want to do- or…or you could join me in a drink in the bar," Raphyl was wearing his inane grin again.

"I think I'll give the drink a rest for one day," Tom said. The two of them walked on in the still air, enveloped in the silence of the plain. The only light now was that which was radiating from the ALSID light bot. Tom wondered whether, had he been out her on his own and had spun around a couple of times, would he lose his bearings completely? Would he know which way he had come or which way he was supposed to be going? He felt comfortable, though, in the midst of the moving pool of light, with his friend and the robot. It was refreshing to be outside of the artificial environment of the station.

Soon, the plot of silent, soft ground beneath their feet gave way to dry, rocky land which crumbled in places as they stepped on the more brittle areas. Tom was careful to watch his footing; he didn't want another injury this far from the station. A tiny blur of pale-yellow light in the distance came into view. Tom wondered what it was. A building perhaps? As they approached it he realised that there was not one but several sources of light and that they were far too small to be buildings. Eventually, he saw that they were glowing rocks; some as small as pebbles, others akin to boulders. Tom was in awe of the beauty of these natural phenomena. Raphyl, however, sauntered on single-mindedly. Tom had the notion that perhaps he was following the smell of alcohol, or whatever that brown drink Truxxians drank was called. They walked on, across the rocky terrain. Suddenly there was a noise. It was coming from the robot. A bleeping mixed with static. Tom whirled around. What was it doing? There was another burst of static and the light went out.

Tom was grateful for the light of the glowing rocks only metres away. He was glad not to be stranded in utter darkness.

"What happened?" he called out.

But Raphyl didn't answer.

In the dimness, Tom saw Raphyl kneel down, reach out and push the octagonal button on the top cube of the robot. A hatchway opened in the side of the lower cube. Raphyl reached inside the hatch.

Tom could see the shadow of a pickaxe in Raphyl's long fingers which he held aloft. What was he doing? Tom backed away, nervously. Why had Tom followed him out here, on an alien planet? He had only known him a few days. What was he doing?

Raphyl stood up slowly, turned to Tom, pickaxe gaining height. Tom didn't like the expression he read on his face; his eyes were narrow, determined. His lips pulled back, jaw wide. Tom gulped. Had the Truxxian brought him out this far into the wastelands to murder him? The pickaxe sliced through the air.

# CHAPTER 13

Tom ducked out of the way and ran. He didn't know where he was heading. He just wanted to get away. Being lost was preferable to being chopped into tiny pieces by a crazed alien.

He could hear incoherent noises behind him as if Raphyl were calling after him, but he continued to run into the darkness, his path lit only by the occasional radiant rock. He briefly rested, hands on his thighs, head low, heart pounding, breathless. Once his pulse had begun to fall, he looked up ahead of him, breathing a little easier. He could see something glistening in the distance. The light was too large to be another boulder. Without looking back, he sped on towards the light.

After a while his legs felt as if they were about to give way beneath him, but he continued, running on pure adrenaline. His body was telling him to stop and rest, but his determination made him proceed towards the light. Relief flooded through him as it became evident that the light was a tall structure.

When he reached the building, he leant against the cool, dark exterior wall. He looked back, panting for air. He couldn't see anything or anyone save for the bright specks of sporadic luminous rocks. He spotted a door close to where he was resting and entered the sanctuary of the building's interior. There was a placard in the warm, inviting reception area in which he found himself. It read *Crossvein Tourist Centre*. Tourist centre? Wasn't Raphyl taking him to somewhere visited by tourists? Why had he come here? This was where Raphyl was heading! But Tom didn't want to go back out into the uncertainty of Truxxe's wilderness – he might get lost and there might not be any other places nearby to hide. He couldn't even lie low and wait for the sunrise, because Truxxe didn't even have a sun. It existed in perpetual darkness. Besides, he was certain that Raphyl was well acquainted with the landscape, so endeavouring to hide out there would be ineffectual.

"Hello, Tom." Tom spun round. It was Phelmer. Tom realised that he must have looked terrified.

"Would you like a drink, Tom?" his wide mouth crept into a reassuring smile. Tom nodded, gratefully. "Right, right." Phelmer placed a long, lilac arm around his exhausted shoulders, paternally, and led him beyond the reception area to a softly lit lounge. He seated Tom gently into a cream ergonomic seat, before gliding over to the bar. Tom sank gladly into the comfort of the seat, feeling his every muscle ache from having been so tense. He looked around him. The environmental settings of the building suggested to him that it was perhaps early afternoon. There was music playing faintly in the background. The place was not nearly as busy as the service station. Tom noticed several Truxxians and beings of other species wearing red robes. He supposed that this must be the uniform worn by the employees here. Some of them were handing out leaflets; others appeared to be leading guided tours through a door on the far wall; others were walking about with trays of food or serving behind the bar. He saw Phelmer being handed two glasses at the bar. His eyes widened. Phelmer. Tom had felt relieved to see a face he recognised, so far from the station, but what if he were no different to Raphyl? After all, Phelmer was the one who had instigated the whole situation – he had been his first point of contact in the entire venture. Tom gulped, but it was too late to run, for he was already on his way back.

"Right we are," Phelmer handed a glass to Tom. "It's only water. You look rather hot and bothered and in need of rehydration." Tom smiled nervously and drank the contents of the glass in one swallow.

"That was perfect, thanks." Phelmer took the seat next to Tom and sipped his own water. His kindly expression put Tom at ease a little. Perhaps his suspicions had been misconceived.

"I must say, I'm surprised that you have hazarded out here on your own, being so new to the planet; did something happen? By the expression on your face earlier, you looked as though you had been chased by a herd of charging Nungbovines!"

"Well," Tom began. "I didn't actually come out here on my own…" After deciding that he would have nothing to lose, he explained to Phelmer what had happened. After he had finished his account, Phelmer raised his monobrow.

"You ran away from Raphyl?" his tone was one of shock.

"Yes," Tom responded. "He was lunging at me with a pickaxe."

"He was actually aiming for you?" Raphyl's expression was calculative.

"Well…" Tom thought for a moment, suddenly feeling slightly foolish. "He was holding it up high and I saw him bring it down but now I come to think of it... I'm not sure whether he was actually *aiming* it at me."

"Tom, I know you are new here. I don't know how much you have learned in the short time you have been on Truxxe, but you do know that all ALSID light bots come equipped with pickaxes don't you?"

"Well, I did see an icon of one on top of the robot, but I thought it was some kind of company branding, I didn't really think anything of it. That was until I saw the thing in Raphyl's hand."

"And you said that the light went out?"

"Yes."

"And did Raphyl then explain to you what had happened?"

"Well, no. He didn't say anything. His manner just changed and his expressions seemed unrecognisable to me..." comprehension dawned on Tom like a dark veil had been lifted from his eyes. "Ah."

"You do realise that..." Phelmer began, gently.

"Yes," Tom interjected. "Because the light had gone out, the ALSID had also ceased to work, therefore I couldn't read Raphyl's expressions... or decipher what he was calling out to me as I was running away." Tom looked down into his vacant glass and rotated it in his hand, swirling the non-existent contents, absentmindedly. "But that doesn't explain about the pickaxe. What would you need one for if not for a weapon?"

"Fuel," Phelmer smiled at him in that smug, but affable way of his. "The ALSID light bot had powered down – it evidently hadn't been fully charged when the two of you had hired it. If there's one thing this planet is useful for, it's fuel. There are so many veins of different types of energy sources here. That's why our planet makes the perfect filling station for so many diverse intergalactic vehicles. This very tourist spot we are in now is a tribute to the richness and diversity of the fuels mined here on Truxxe. You can take the guided tour if you wish to delve into the history of the planet."

"But what about the pickaxe?" Tom asked, impatiently.

"You undoubtedly saw the glowing stones on your journey?" Tom nodded. "And did you notice that they emit the same level of light as the ALSID light bot? The same hue? The same intensity?"

"Er..."

"Well those stones are the fuel for the robots. You only need hack away a chunk of one of those rocks and it will feed an ALSID bot for half a rotation or more."

"So *that's* what the pickaxe is for," Tom looked up and into the friendly lilac face. Phelmer's gaze focussed on something behind him. Tom turned around. Raphyl was standing behind him.

"Drinking without me, Tombo?"

Phelmer had left the two colleagues to talk and was speaking with someone else over by the bar. Tom felt awkward, but he was also glad that the ordeal had simply been a misunderstanding. Raphyl had bought them both carbonated fruit drinks and a bowl of green nuts each and was sitting in the plush cream seat opposite him.

"I'm sorry, Raphyl. That's twice I've done that now. I don't know what it is… I think I just kind of… panic."

"Hey that's all right, I should have warned you that the robot might shut down at any moment. There's no fuel gauge on the things – I told you they like to cut costs."

"Maybe, but I should have realised that it was a communications machine and that if the light had gone out then the translation system would be down as well. It's just when I saw you with that pickaxe in your hand coming at me in the darkness…"

"There was a rock right behind you, Tom. It was perfect – had a good crumbly bit just big enough for the fuel chamber. I didn't realise you were scared – that's not the expression I read from you. Just goes to show how much we rely on the ALSID units, eh? Anyway, sorry I took so long getting here. It's not easy lugging those bots around. I know they hover, but they can only go a certain speed. Really annoying. I'm glad you found Phelmer and that you're OK anyway," said Raphyl and took a swig from his glass. "You want to have a look around then?"

"All right." Tom followed Raphyl to the door where the guided tours were being led. He showed his card to an attendant who was clad in the red uniform. The attendant opened the door obligingly. "There you go, free admission. These cards have some perks."
"Where do I get one?"

"You'll probably be issued one after your first week. Go on then." Raphyl gestured towards the door. Tom hesitated.

"Aren't you coming in, then?"

"Me? Nah, I've been round plenty of times – bores the compshoes off me. I'll wait for you in the bar." Raphyl grinned and waved at Tom as he went on through alone.

He found himself in a huge chamber. The roof was domed and a walkway ran around the edge. Tom walked over to the railing in front of him and discovered that a drop of several metres lay below, occupying most of the circular room. He stepped back. He noticed several tourists dotted along the walkway, stopping at intervals to view something at recesses in the wall along their journey. He could hear a faint commentary echoing throughout the chamber, although he could not make out what was being said. He decided he may as well look around while he was here and followed the route around the chamber in a counterclockwise direction. He soon came to the first recess which lit up automatically as he stepped in front of it. The system reminded Tom of a visit to a museum when he was at school, where there had been exhibitions of rocks, dinosaur bones and old weaponry. However, instead of a display of Earthly artefacts, he was presented with a planetary globe; a three-dimensional map of Truxxe. It was very different to the globes of Earth. Tom examined it in fascination as it spun demonstratively on its axis. A disembodied male voice echoed around him.

"Truxxe, the wandering planetoid," it began. "Spinning in the cosmos, its unique perpetual rotation a mystery to scientists today." As the model Truxxe spun, Tom could see channels of different surface colours and textures. He thought back to his and Raphyl's journey to the Crossvein Tourist Centre. He remembered having walked on the soft, earthy soil and then the sudden change to the hard, rocky terrain and then they had come across the light-emitting rocks. The information he was hearing and the map in front of him supported his experience. However, when he looked more closely, Tom realised that the jumble of land-type was chiefly evident in the northern hemisphere. The bottom third of the planetoid was one dark rocky hue with little water that Tom could see. In the northern hemisphere there were large bodies of water, although nothing like the ratio of that on Earth. The voice went on, "Historians conclude that our bounty of resources is thanks to numerous collisions with other planets – this would certainly explain the variety of terrain. Our neighbouring building, Truxxe Superior

Services, is the planet's main fuel supplier to off-world transportation, its location being central to many of the northern mines." The light went out and the voice ceased. Tom took this as his cue to continue along the walkway. After a dozen metres or so, his motion triggered another display. A close-up holographic view of the terrain was displayed in the recess and Tom could make out two distinctive buildings on the map. The disembodied voice continued, "Here is a close-up view of the immediate area. The large building on the right is Truxxe Superior Services. On the left; Crossvein. You will notice that there are eight definite crystalline plains which meet to the east of this centre. Fuel mined in these plains includes coal, oil, silicate and magma. Due north of the site lies twenty-square miles of geysers…" Tom decided that he had had enough of his geology lesson and moved along, leaving the voice talking away to itself. The next exhibit showed holograms of miners, one of the main occupations on Truxxe. The commentary explained the history of the craft and various methods used to extract the material throughout the ages. The next session mentioned, briefly, the southern hemisphere, which had fewer mines and didn't have the benefit of the tourist industry brought by the service station port. The images portrayed beings in drab clothing - all Truxxians. They appeared to be living in small dwellings, in squalor almost. The commentary then seemed to gloss over this poignant element and went on to explain how the northern hemisphere had become such an enterprising place; having reached its reputable interplanetary status a century ago and rendered images of happy, healthy inhabitants; nurses, captains, chefs, labourers. But Tom had stopped listening to the boastful exploits – he couldn't get the image of the destitution of those other inhabitants out of his head. His brain started to fill in the missing pieces. Why had the exhibition belittled the reasons for their poverty? Surely it was lack of water and good soil for crops? And the lack of fuel variety for miners? Tom shivered, cursing his own ignorance of the planet's politics and left the chamber. He came back into the subdued lighting and soft music of the bar area. Raphyl was looking comfortable and reposed, slouching in one of the cream seats sipping a glass of thick brown gloop. He was talking to someone, a female, who smiled and waved at Raphyl as she walked away.

"See you in a bit, Nowrella," he called after her casually. He looked as though he had had several of his opaque, brown drinks in the short time Tom had been absent. For some reason this made Tom feel angry. The comparable luxury of this building and the decadence of it all, juxtaposed to the exhibits portraying the barrenness and filth he had seen in that snapshot of life on the other side of Truxxe made him feel enraged. How could they let it happen? "That was quick, enjoy the exhibition?" Tom glared at him.

"It was… interesting," Tom said through gritted teeth and plopped down, hoping that the softness of the moulding chair would help calm him.

"You weren't bored to death then?" Raphyl smiled, he looked as though he was having trouble focussing on him.

"Not exactly," he took a deep breath. "Do you like living on Truxxe, Raphyl?"

"It's all right I suppose… It's where I grew up," he said, indifferently. "I haven't been to many planets, but it's not bad." He took another sip.

"The exhibition – it mentioned the South. Have you ever been there?"

"Oh," Raphyl's expression appeared almost sober. "I'd forgotten about that part – been a while since I've been round and had a proper look at the demonstration." He looked at his timepiece and added, "We'd better go, it's getting pretty late, isn't it? We do have to get up early for work and it's a long walk back." Tom was frustrated by Raphyl's lack of a satisfactory reply. And he was surprised at his sudden concern about the time. He wasn't usually so worried about work.

"What about your friend?" Tom nodded in the direction of the female he had been talking to her who was now talking with another girl at the bar.

"Oh," Raphyl hesitated, as if he were having an inner battle. "Umm… I'll talk to her another time." He finished his drink. "Let's go and get the robot and go back, shall we?"

The journey back didn't take as long as Tom had anticipated, despite having run half of the distance on the trip there. Raphyl was talking. A lot. It was as though he didn't want Tom to have chance to ask him about the images he had seen in the exhibition. He talked about everything from burger relish to intergalactic Spotoon championship matches. His babble reminded Tom of Nathan and how he had used to let his tongue rattle when he had been drinking too. But this time Tom wasn't amused. He was too busy thinking about those people in the images, their emaciated faces, their shabby homes. His thoughts turned to his home planet and how so many people there were suffering too, in the developing world. He realised that he had put it out of his mind a lot of the time. Maybe Raphyl was doing the same with those hungry people on Truxxe, although Tom didn't yet comprehend how deep the truth, in Raphyl, really lay.

# CHAPTER 14

When Tom entered the Express Cuisine restaurant the following morning, he could sense that Miss Lolah was somewhere in the vicinity. He could feel the intensity of the emotions her pheromone field was stirring inside him. Jambole Farr walked with him on his way to the kitchen area. The green, lizard-skinned man was laughing.

"Are you looking for the supervisor?"

"I was just wandering where she was." He tried to sound casual, but he found himself longing to gaze into the darkness of her camera lens again. He silently cursed these invasive thoughts.

"I must admit, after all these years I'm not immune to it, but your reaction makes me laugh – it's the same with Raphyl. It's as if it's particularly strong for younger men."

"That's because they need to be encouraged to work harder, the younger they are," Kayleesh said abruptly, scowling across the room as Raphyl sauntered in with his usual idle gait. Tom laughed. Kayleesh broke into a giggle. Tom found that he was suddenly standing up straight and had an urge to impress – he looked around, trying to determine who the first customer might be. Perhaps he could have the first go at serving today.

"Tom Bowler," a voice like melting honey reached his ear. He turned around. The bronze, boxy robot was standing in front of him. His gaze fell involuntarily down her long, metallic neck. He took control of his eyes and forced his glance upwards. The mechanical sound of the lens as it focussed on him was as captivating as a love song as he looked at the metal grille of the speaker; anticipating the next beautiful words to sound out from it. He was sure he could hear Jambole snigger as he disappeared behind the shelving and into the kitchen area, but he didn't care. He wasn't important. At this moment, only Miss Lolah was important.

"I'm glad you're feeling better today," she said. Her programming made her glad that he was here. Tom smiled, eyes glazed over. He was glad too. "As you might know, Maytey Reeston is still in the Clinicarium – therefore we're still one short. Instead of working alongside Raphyl today, I'd like you to help out with some of Maytey's usual duties. I don't expect you to carry out any of the light maintenance jobs he does but if you could keep the place orderly it would help us out, today." Tom nodded enthusiastically, like a small child being asked if they wanted to lick the cake mixture from the mixing bowl. "Good," the robot said benevolently. "You will find the relevant cleaning materials in the cleaning cupboard over there." A metal arm clunked two distinctive notches upwards until it was pointing, at shoulder height, to the robot's right. Miss Lolah lowered her arm and walked awkwardly away on her metallic legs, in the direction of her office. Once out of the influence of the pherobot's field, Tom realised what he had agreed to. He ignored Kayleesh's laughter and walked over to the cleaning cupboard.

Hannond Putt pulled on the blue uniform with which he had been provided. It was a waterproof airtight affair, rather than the flowing blue robes he had seen the employees wearing in the upper floors. He regarded the purple TSS logo on his rounded front and touched it with a chunky grey finger. He felt almost proud to wear a uniform baring such a well-respected motif; then he remembered why he was here. This was only a temporary position and he was only here to collect the fully formed Glorbian gems. He had already met his supervisor, Miss Monah, and had found the experience rather overwhelming. He had heard of pherobots - his father had mentioned them once or twice when he used to tell them about his travels - but Hannond would never have understood wholly had he not met one for himself. He was glad to have his own thoughts back, however, so that he could focus properly on his own mission. He had been assigned to work in the preliminary filter zone - much to Hannond's relief for this was the most likely section where the gems would collect. Although the relief he felt was short-lived, because he soon discovered that he would not be working alone when he was greeted by a plump, white being from planet Strellion. Strellions are notoriously nosy and Hannond knew instantly that keeping his secret business a secret was not going to be an easy feat. The Strellion towered over the three-foot high Glorbian. His uniform was stretched to its maximum over his large frame. He was covered in white downy fur, although Hannond predicted that it would be dank, brown fur by the end of the shift. His nose protruded a good foot from his body, which he insisted on sniffing through loudly as frequent intervals; another unfortunate feature to possess when working with sewage.

"Hello, I'm Eto," he greeted Hannond. His voice was deep. Eto looked down at him and was standing so close that his great nose was practically resting on Hannond's head. Hannond took a step back before introducing himself.

"I'm Hannond."

"Nice to meet you, Hannond. We're one short on our Spotoon team - would you like to join?"

Tom was wandering around the restaurant with the broom he had seen Maytey use. He was almost disappointed that there wasn't a great deal of debris of which to collect in the transparent tube. He was wondering about the coins, which then led him to think about money. This was his fourth working day. True, he had been off sick the day before, but he only had three more days until he would receive his wages. He would have to reimburse Raphyl for the money he had lent him for the compsuit and the timepiece. He also owed him several drinks. He wondered how much he would have left to spend after his lodgings had been deducted. Other than buying some proper meals and the occasional night out, Tom hoped that he could somehow use his money to contact his parents and his friend and cousin on Earth. He imagined telling Nathan and Max about Truxxe and all the alien beings he had met and of all the customs he had observed. He wished that he could visit them. *I wonder how long I would have to work here to be able to afford my own spaceship?* He laughed to himself. He absentmindedly swept under one of the vacant tables. Tom could hear part of a conversation between two of the praying-mantis creatures at an adjacent table.

"So, how are we going to prove that the original theory is false?" one of them was saying.

"Well, nobody has ever proved that it was true in the first place - it is just a *theory*."

"Or a cover up," agreed the first speaker. Tom strained to hear the next part as the speaker's voice lowered to a whisper. He continued to sweep the same bit of floor. "But what would someone have to gain by engineering the whole thing? *The whole planet?* They must have gone to great lengths, whoever it was. And they must have had a lot of time."

"You forget that some entities have life spans far greater than ours. Or perhaps it's not just the plot of one person – perhaps it's the work of several generations. And what would they have to gain, you ask? Why - the place is a goldmine!" Tom surreptitiously edged his way in the direction of the occupied table, apparently following his broom and minding his own business. He was intrigued. What plot were they talking about? What planet? He swept around the single leg of the turquoise table. There was something on the table. He glanced at it – a map. He tried to make out the detail without seeming too obvious. He recognised it. It was a map of Truxxe. There were annotations around the edge and crossings out, but he could not make them out. Suddenly, the handle of his broom caught the edge of the table, causing a full milkshake carton to spill its contents over the table. And over the map. Tom put his hand to his mouth in horror and dropped the broom handle.

"I am *so* sorry," he said sincerely. Two sets of insectile eyes glared at him from underneath their hooded tops.

"That was a very important document!" One of them bellowed.

"I'm sorry, I'll clean it up," Tom headed for the cleaning supplies cupboard.

"Don't worry," the other one called after him. "I can draw up another one. Just fetch me a cloth for the table and another milkshake." When he returned, Tom's shoulders fell as he saw that the map had gone. He mopped up the spillage, feeling the two customers glowering at him as he did so before he went to order a replacement drink. Tom kept his distance from that particular table while they continued to dine and busied himself wiping vacant tables at the other end of the restaurant. Once they had left, Tom kept glancing over at where Raphyl was working. He wanted to tell him what he had seen but he seemed to have an endless stream of customers queuing up to order food. Tom didn't want to slow the queue even more by distracting his friend – he didn't want to annoy any more customers. As the shift neared its end, Tom's legs were aching from standing for so long and he was bored of the tedium of Maytey's job. He hoped that Maytey would return to work soon. Yawning, he tidied the broom away and handed a stack of soiled cloths over to a bemused Jephle in the kitchen to be washed. He had watched Maytey empty the several bins, which were dotted around the eating area, at the end of previous shifts so he took a refuse sack from the cupboard and began filling it with the contents of the first bin. Amongst the empty drinks cartons and food wrappings, he noticed a large sheet of paper. Tom's stomach lurched with excitement – it was the map. He looked around him for any onlookers before reaching into the bin. He pulled out the soggy, crumpled map before folding it and placing it in the deep pocket of his uniform.

# CHAPTER 15

Tom was in the comfort and privacy of his own quarters. He was seated at the table in one of the blue chairs which soothed his aching muscles as he relaxed into it. He had the map in his hands. He had cleaned off as much ruffleberry milkshake as he could, although parts of it were still illegible. He traced his finger along the map as he considered it. The map, he recognised, was of the northern hemisphere. He could identify some of the patterns of varying land-types from the spinning globe he had seen in the tourist centre. He smoothed out the creases with his hands and inspected the comments around the edge of the document.

*Why does Truxxe have so many different resources? Historians dictate that this phenomenon is due to collisions with other planets, but what is the chance of this many resourceful planets having collided with the molten core of Truxxe? Millions to one? If, however, it occurred by an external force then how?* There were further lines underneath, however the page was too soiled for Tom to make out anymore of the words. He was confused. Someone was questioning the information which he had learned only yesterday at the tourist centre; those praying mantis creatures. Why were they so interested in the genuine history of the planet? Would it change things if the story he knew to be true was a cover-up? Tom didn't know but what he wanted to know was why they were so inquisitive – why were they so enraged that the map had been spoiled? There was a knock on the door. He remembered that he and Raphyl had planned to go to Six Seven. He folded the map carefully and put it into the pocket of his compsuit.

Tom, Raphyl and Kayleesh were sitting in a cloistered corner of the busy recreational room Bar Six Seven. Tom had guardedly shown his friends the annotated map and was asking their opinions. Raphyl seemed characteristically indifferent about the matter.

"What are you getting so worked up about, Tom? It's only the scribblings of a couple of nutcases. It's not exactly proof. And even if it was – who cares?" Raphyl took a swig of his brown beverage, unperturbed.

"I think it could be important, Tom," Kayleesh said excitedly. "I have heard about these conspiracy theories before – whoever wrote this is not alone in their thinking."

"Really? What do you know?" Tom turned to her, expectantly. Kayleesh took a sip of her carbonated fruit drink and her expression suggested she was working out where best to begin.

"Well, my father didn't want me to come and work here, you know. He had heard about the contrast of the wealthy two-thirds and the poverty-stricken south. This disharmony is so unlike that of Augtopia that the idea of it offended him. Augtopia is not the richest of worlds by any means – in fact the living conditions are rather harsh, but we have a notorious culture of sharing. Anyway, he had heard of the speculations that the planet was engineered this way."

"Why would it be purposefully engineered this way?" Tom was confused. He glanced over at Raphyl who was leaning back in his chair and glancing around room. He turned back to Kayleesh.

"I don't *know* why, Tom. But my father agreed with the idea that it's too much of a coincidence that a planetoid such as this exists in nature – what is the chance that all these planets rich in these fuels should collide and that it exists here – in this geographical position. So far away from any other planet – or even the nearest galaxy! You have to admit that it is rather suspicious." Tom was pleased that Kayleesh was interested in his findings, that there was more to it than he had originally thought. He thought it best not to mention about the poverty on his own planet and prompted further.

"Yes, it does all seem rather… convenient," Tom agreed. He looked at the crumpled map in his lap and thought about the hungry faces on the Truxxians in the exhibition hologram. He looked around the room at the smiling, drinking, chatting beings of many races. The set-up was wonderfully convenient – he had learned about the fortunate positioning and structure of the planet as far back as his interview with Tyrander, but if the whole place was created then where did destitution come into the equation? He wanted Raphyl's opinion – surely it meant something to him? He had not asked him before but now that he had this new piece of evidence – the map – and Kayleesh's testimony then it all seemed more significant somehow. Perhaps Raphyl knew more than he was disclosing.

"Raphyl, aren't you interested? Have you heard about the conspiracy before?" Tom asked. Raphyl turned to him, his expression a little irritated.

"No, I'm *not* interested. Can't we talk about something else?"

"But it's your home planet. Don't you want to know the truth?" asked Tom. Raphyl stood up.

"Yes, it *is* my home planet so it's none of your business," he snapped and proceeded to march across the room and out of the door.

"He *must* have been annoyed," Tom noted. "He left half of his drink." He turned to Kayleesh who had her head in her hands. "What?" he asked. Kayleesh raised her head slowly.

"I've just realised. I mean, I could be wrong, but,"

"But what?" Tom looked into her deep violet eyes.

"I think he's from the south."

Tom's mind was running a marathon around his skull. "What do you mean? Did he tell you?"

"No." Kayleesh twirled a piece of her golden hair around a finger, nervously. "I think that's why he won't talk about it. I think he feels guilty for living up here."

"But, why?"

Kayleesh gave a half shrug. "Perhaps he left his family behind. Who knows? It's obviously something personal like that or he wouldn't have acted in that way." How had she deduced this information? Perhaps it was because she was a girl, Tom mused. Girls were strange like that. He wondered if her speculation was correct. "I'll go after him." He stood up. Kayleesh followed suit but, to his disappointment, she wasn't going to join him.

"I've spotted someone I know," she pointed towards a group of girls near the bar. "I'll see you at work tomorrow." She smiled at him and left the table. Tom made his way out of the door and looked down the corridor. There were several employees around but none of them were Raphyl. He made his way hurriedly to the lift and stepped inside. In his haste he let the arrow on the trackball of the lift control rest on thirty-three in error. *Oh no I meant thirty-two. Thirty-two.* But the lift had already begun its ascent. He thumped the wall in frustration. Tom waited as the lift unknowingly made its journey to the incorrect floor. When it arrived, there was someone waiting to board. It was a large, green being whose foul breath he could smell from the moment the doors had slid open. Tom looked up and into the furious features of Baff Bulken.

Tom reached for the lift controls, but it was too late. Baff lugged his weighty frame into the lift and the door hummed mockingly behind him, rendering Tom trapped. Baff pressed a great sweaty hand on Tom's, preventing him from adjusting the trackball. Baff's angered expression was now one of amusement. Tom felt as though he were a cat's plaything. He didn't know where to look other than into that great green face and at the thick yellow saliva which was seeping into the brown facial hair under Baff's lower lip.

"Where are your team mates to protect you now, human? You can't hide behind any furniture in here." Baff's rancid, malicious toothy grin widened. Tom screwed up his face in repulsion at the stench of his fetid breath. He struggled desperately to stop himself from puking from both the odour and from fear. He put his free hand to his mouth, feeling his half-digested burger meal rising involuntarily up his gullet.

"What are you doing?" Baff's expression was one of puzzlement. His words liberated more of the noxious-smelling gas of the creature's sour breath. Tom couldn't speak. His eyes were watering. He could hold it in no longer. He dropped his hand from his face and clutched his abdomen. His stomach lurched as its contents detonated over Baff Bulken's vast front in a huge explosion of vomit. To Tom's horror, the soup-like substance on Baff's chest began hissing and spitting like an egg frying in hot fat. His compsuit was beginning to smoulder. Baff recoiled in horror, his hand finally releasing his. Tom swiftly dialled the correct level, his insides churning and his mind racing. The lift made its short passage to the floor below and Tom left, leaving the rival Spotoon player slouched in the corner of the lift, covered in Tom's vomit. He sprinted down the corridor without looking back, racing towards his apartment. When he arrived, breathless, he let himself in, shut the door and slumped to the floor. The feeling of sickness had not subsided. He took in long, deep breaths. He couldn't think straight. He was relieved to be out of the situation and in the refuge of his own quarters again, but what if one of the BBs were to come after him again? He wouldn't be safe forever. And why did his vomit have that effect on Baff Bulken? What had it done to him? He gulped, his mind conjuring up consequences to his predicament. What if he had killed him and they locked Tom away in a secure unit somewhere on the station for his crime? What if he could never get home again? He felt a sudden homesickness. This place was too unpredictable. He would never get used to it. Even Raphyl was acting strangely towards him now. Perhaps it would be best for everyone if he went home.

# CHAPTER 16

Tom was dreaming about Earth. He was dreaming about the day he had received his exam results and he was celebrating with Nathan and his other classmates. They were at their local, which was bursting with students; either rejoicing or commiserating. Max had joined his cousin to buy congratulatory drinks for Tom and his friends. They were laughing, reminiscing and singing discordantly. He noticed a group of people over where the dartboard was. They were throwing ordinary darts, but the dartboard was not there – there was something in its place. None of his friends remarked on this, they simply continued their jovial conversation and tuneless crooning. Tom stepped slowly towards the oche. What were they aiming at? There was something bloody pegged to the cork-backed wall. As he approached, he realised what they were aiming at. There, nailed to the wall was Tom's own head. A dart whizzed past Tom's ear and pierced the left eye of the disembodied face. There were whoops of elation from whoever had thrown it. Tom turned in horror to see that the purveyor was a smirking, dribbling Baff Bulken.

*Paaaaaaaaaaaaaaaaaarp!* The alarm broke his dream. Tom was in his quarters, in bed, fully clothed. The room fell silent. He could hear only his own panicked breathing. He wandered what became of Baff after he had left him in the lift the previous evening. He wandered if news of the event had spread to the rest of the team. Had Tom's colleagues found out? What about police - there must be some kind of law enforcement on Truxxe. Tom pulled the covers over his head – he wanted to make the most of being in under-rated ignorant bliss for a while longer. *Paaaaaaaaaaaaaaaaarp!* The alarm sounded its second blast. Reluctantly he crawled out of bed and then prepared himself for work at a lethargic pace.

Once he had reached the lift at the end of the passageway, Tom ensured that he didn't enter it alone and looked anxiously about him. Everything seemed normal so far. There was no evidence that anything gruesome had occurred; no vomit residue or molten Baff plastered on walls. People were talking amongst themselves in their usual manner. There were several early morning yawns – nothing out of the ordinary. He made his routine journey from the foyer to his workplace.

"I didn't realise humans had a defence mechanism," Maytey grinned at him as Tom approached his workstation.

"What do you mean?" asked Tom carefully.

"Apparently you threw up on Bulken – very brave," Raphyl said ominously.

"How did you find out?"

"One of the other dribblers happened to find him. The information must have filtered through the whole team before it got to Hasprin's Legion." Tom bit his lip.

"Is… is he all right?"

"Is he *all right?* What are you worried about that for Tom? If you hadn't have done what you did he would have *pounded* you," Maytey said, sounding a little exasperated.

"Well it's not like I had a lot of choice," admitted Tom, the uncomfortable feeling in his stomach returning.

"So you didn't know that his species were intolerant to stomach acid?" asked Maytey.

"No. It just… happened. I just felt sick. I was scared and… well… his breath was *evil*."

"Not as evil as his punches," warned Raphyl.

"So, is he all right? Will I get into trouble?"

"No you won't, and he'll be fine – I'm sure he's suffering from shock more than anything." Maytey rested a reassuring hand on his shoulder. "His reputation has been tainted and you've probably removed a layer of his skin and ruined his compsuit that's all." Tom gulped. "Don't worry – I'm sure he'll stay away from you for a while," Maytey added with a half-convincing smile. But Tom *was* worried. The thought of an even angrier Baff terrified him. Surely he wouldn't be satisfied with the rumour of being beaten by a member of a rival team; a much smaller member at that. Before he could get tied up in his ruminations any further, he felt the now familiar awareness that Miss Lolah had entered into the locality. Her soft feminine voice resonated from behind them.

"Please take your posts, everyone."

Raphyl did not mention the previous night regarding his storming out of Six Seven, preferring instead to ask Tom to recount his experience with Baff several times over, demanding every detail. Tom really wanted nothing more than to forget the whole encounter, but he was just glad that Raphyl was speaking to him again and happily met his requests. The day was relatively uneventful and Tom served most of the customers himself while his colleague willingly stepped back. As the shift neared its end, conversation developed into talk about Earth. Tom had not yet spoken much about Earth to his new friends and Raphyl showed more interested than Tom had imagined. He told him about his friends, his house, his old school, television, music and the weather. He even told him about motorway service stations and their resemblance to TSS although Raphyl found this concept amusing and pointless. He thought it peculiar that only natives were known to live on Tom's home planet. Raphyl was curious about the seasons, and the natural dawning and setting of the sun, as he had never experienced such things for himself.

"Raphyl, I know I've only been here a few rotations but is there any way I can get back to Earth – I mean just to visit?" Tom asked.

"It's not like you can hop onto a ship that happens to be going to your planet, Tombo," Raphyl said sincerely.

"No... I suppose not. If only I could speak to my friends – just to let them know how I'm doing." A slow smile spread across Raphyl's lilac face.

"Oh, well that you *can* do."

"What? You mean I can talk to them?"

"Yes and *see* them. And they'll be able to see you too," Raphyl smiled.

"Really? How?"

"Well... long-distance calls are expensive... but as soon as we get paid, I'll take you to use the holoceiver. We can book a session if you like." Raphyl's eyes widened at the apparent prospect.

"The what?" Why hadn't Tom heard about this before?

"You can contact whoever you want to talk to and the holoceiver will project your image."

"You mean... I can project an image of *me* into my house back on Earth?"

"Yes, that's right," said Raphyl. Tom contemplated the idea.

"Will they know that it's a projection? I mean... my family don't know..."

"The resolution in the newer models is pretty impressive so they shouldn't be able to tell you're a hologram. Unless…"

"Unless what?"

"Unless they try to touch you of course."

Tom detected Raphyl's amusement as he felt his face redden again. He was sure that his mother's first reaction would be to hug him. He imagined his mother leaning forward to wrap her arms around her son; her son whom she had not seen for over a week and was so fond of. He imagined her horror as her hands passed instead through empty space. He couldn't let that happen – she'd either think he had come to visit her from the dead or he would have to tell her the truth and he didn't like the prospect of either. He would have to think of a way to prevent anyone from touching him.

"So, shall I show you how to book a call?" Raphyl asked him. He obviously noticed the confusion on Tom's face because he added, "You can't just go along and use the holoceiver you know, you have to book in advance. It's a popular contraption."

Tom nodded. "I suppose it would be!"

After they had eaten their post-shift meal with the other employees, Raphyl took Tom to one of the complex's ground floor rooms which were open to both staff members and visitors. Tom hadn't been down that particular district of the main floor before and was amazed at the enormity of the place and the variety of services on offer. They passed a huge array of boutiques, eating-places, lounges and bars. They came to a halt outside a retail outlet with a green hologram sign above the door which was projected a good foot away from the wall. It read *Holoceiver Exchange*. Underneath, in smaller type, it read *Special rates on inter-planetary calls*.

"Hey, I might be able to get a good deal!" Tom pointed enthusiastically at the sign.

"They only say that to get you interested," explained Raphyl. "They're the only company in the whole centre that offers this service so…"

"So I bet they still charge the Earth," finished Tom.

"The Earth?" Raphyl looked puzzled.

Tom laughed and shook his head, dismissively. "It doesn't matter. OK let's book it anyway." The square reception room was decorated in the shade of pale green usually reserved for doctor's waiting rooms. To support this unintentional theme, a row of occupied seats ran along the right-hand wall. Ahead of Tom and Raphyl was a single door with the word *Engaged* in green holographic lettering above it. A low desk spanned the wall to their left, behind which sat a small creature, which had the appearance of a distorted faceless yellow bubble. The delicate creature shifted and bobbed around in its ergonomic seat. The semi-transparent yellow receptionist was still somehow sporting a blue employee's uniform although it seemed viscous and appeared to ripple and swell in unison with the bubble-formed body as it moved. When the receptionist addressed them, the voice was liquid and androgynous.

"Can I help you?" Tom heard in plain English, but the words reverberated somewhere in his mind and didn't seem to come from any particular direction. Tom sensed that it wasn't sound that was being emitted, but some kind of telepathic correspondence. Perhaps it was being translated by the ALSID unit. He was still uncomfortable with the idea of his brain being directly contacted, scanned or otherwise interfered with.

"Yes. Could I book a holoceiver... er... session?" Tom said out loud, a little unsure of the expected terminology. The bubble-creature responded to his vocal request, again telepathically.

"Yes. The waiting list is currently two rotations. Is the sixth hour suitable?"

"Yes, great!" Tom thought that he could see the bubble ebb and flow in its seat and then it heaved its warping upper body. He watched as something solid and white appeared to be forming inside it. He looked at Raphyl for a reaction, but he was looking inattentively around the room. He turned back to the receptionist and saw that the solid shape was growing; an animated envelope unfolding amidst the glutinous body. It reminded Tom of the customer he had seen digesting a meal, except that this creature looked hollow and full of air rather than jelly. Furthermore, it seemed to be performing the reverse action as the unfurling object was being pushed upwards and outwards. Slowly, slowly, the article was driven further upwards and outwards until Tom was sure that the corners of the item were going to burst the bubble from the inside. However, it passed through with ease so that three-quarters of the item was flapping about in the open air, like a letter sticking out of a letter box.

"Go on, take it," Raphyl instructed. Tom raised an eyebrow but didn't say anything. He reached across and grabbed hold of the paper. It was unexpectedly dry and substantial considering he had seen it ostensibly grow from nothing. He winced as he pulled the sheet the whole way out. *What am I doing?*

"Er... thanks," he managed and fixed his eyes on the sheet of paper so that he could avoid looking at the faceless being from which the paper had been pulled. The details of Tom's appointment were printed onto it, the day, time, even his name. He didn't remember giving his name. He shuddered at the thought of his thoughts being read by this telepathic transparent yellow being and then wondered if it could detect his mixed feelings of fascination and repulsion? He decided to leave, quickly, before his thoughts got him into trouble.

Later that evening, Ghy Hasprin had rounded up his now-recovered teammates who were occupying an oval-shaped table in Six Seven. It was comfortably warm, and the strange rock folk music was playing several decibels louder than usual. Tom found that he now recognised one or two of the underlying melodies and found himself occasionally humming along. Ghy had brought everyone a drink to celebrate their reunion after their brief break and had announced that he had gathered the team for a friendly game against the Gharka. Tom peered over his tripedal glass at the opposing team. One of them looked to Tom like the mythological abominable snowman with a nose the size of a marrow. He was by far the tallest of the team and tufts of long, dirty, white fur were sticking out of the gaps in his compsuit. He recognised the species of the smallest member of the team, a flash of recollection from the man he had seen unloading the Cluock supply ship. He also recognised the same odour which he had detected on that delivery day. Perhaps they all smelled that way, he mused. There were three other less remarkable-looking members; a Truxxian, and two others who had their backs to him so that Tom couldn't yet see their faces. The tall, hairy white creature approached the table where Hasprin's team was sitting. Tom rested his drink on the table.

"Hello Hasprin," he addressed Ghy, his great nose directly above Tom's head. "I'd like to introduce our new team member - Hannond Putt." Tom looked up and saw that the large being was grinning and pointing at the short smelly creature, who was being commandeered to the table by the Truxxian team member. The stumpy, brown-haired, grey-skinned being padded towards Hasprin's Legion. Tom saw that Hannond had deep blue placid eyes and looked as though he were perhaps several years younger than the deliveryman in the Cluock. He wondered whether this new member was as naïve as Tom had been on joining a Spotoon team. He thought of Baff Bulken and was glad that they weren't playing his team tonight.

"Nice to meet you Hannond," Ghy said, genuinely. "OK let's have a game." He stood up and the team followed him to join the rest of the Gharka in the game area. The Gharka let their newest member step up first and he projected an impressive bullet-like mass of sputum onto the disc in the red ring, which ran around the perimeter of the green central zone. Ghy angled his ear in Hannond's direction politely and smiled but said nothing. Ghy stepped forward and his spittle landed precisely in the centre of the green area. A member of the opposing team took his turn and managed to also score within the green zone. As Tom took his place for his own turn, he could see a familiar face in the corner of his vision. It was Kayleesh, her blonde hair shining in the soft ambience of the room. Tom paused, realising that his mouth was dry. How could he compete in this sport with a dry mouth? As if she had read his thoughts, Kayleesh picked up Tom's distinguishable alcoholic drink from the table and handed it to him. Her eyes were twinkling as she smiled at him.

"Need a drop of this, Tom?" Tom thanked her, took a gulp and handed it back to her. For a moment Tom thought that perhaps Kayleesh had a telepathic nature like the bubble-creature he had met, then he realised that it was more likely that she had simply got to know Tom and his impulses. Nathan would have acted in the same way, given the circumstance. But Tom thought of Kayleesh as *more* than a friend and the more he thought about this in those few moments before he took his turn, the more nervous he became. He was aware of her soft eyes on him as he readied himself for his shot at the disc. He shifted uncomfortably at the chalked line, tried to produce a fair amount of saliva. In a bid to accelerate this moment of awkwardness he rushed his turn and failed to properly aim, causing the spittle to miss the disc completely. He turned and instead of the look of amazement he longed to see in her eyes, he detected an expression of pity. He hung his head, shamefully and avoided looking at the rest of his teammates.

"Bad luck, Tom," he heard Ghy say. "Try not to let yourself get too… distracted." Tom felt his face redden. He wished he hadn't noticed Kayleesh was there when he had, then perhaps he would have scored as high as Ghy. Why was she making him feel so nervous? He was sure that she never used to have this effect on him. Tom endeavoured to concentrate on the game on his subsequent shots. He managed to improve his aim, although he fell short of his usual high scoring. Hasprin's Legion finished in first place. Tom found the scoring system for Spotoon rather confusing and it had taken him several games to actually understand how the winner was determined. Tom understood the rules to be that it was only really the green inner circle which counted, no matter the combination of shots on the outer rings. He let the team captains pronounce the winning team, although he could understand how the situation could get confusing and fights could start. Tom thought that perhaps a numbered system would be more appropriate, as though it were a basic darts game, with a different figure for each ring. Once, he had discussed this with Kayleesh, judging that she would be less likely to laugh at his suggestion than an experienced Spotoon player from his team. She had smiled and stated that the game was originally designed for males whose jobs required little or no brainpower, therefore the need for numerical skills was not desirable for their leisure activities. Tom had not been sure how to take this comment initially but had decided that it couldn't have been an insult to his occupation because she also worked in the express cuisine restaurant. She may have been clever, but she was in the same situation as him.

At home, Tom had been known for being the pupil who came top of his class; the teenager who spent too much time in front of his computer or with his head in a book. He wandered how people saw him here? His lifestyle had changed, certainly. Was he fitting in? Tom had never worried about fitting in before and had always felt comfortable with his small group of friends, working hard and playing hard. He laughed at the irony that he might actually fit it better with an alien society than in his hometown where he had lived for eighteen years.

For the next two days Tom thought about using the holoceiver. He was looking forward to seeing his family again, but he was apprehensive, too. What could he talk to them about? He would have to be economical with the truth and regulate his stories of his new job and his new life. And he had to prevent his family from trying to hug him. He had thought about pretending he had a cold, but he knew that wouldn't stop his adoring mother from holding her son in her arms. He would have to pretend it was something worse. But then she would insist that he stay at home with them until the illness had passed. Tom also spent a lot of time thinking about Kayleesh. She had come to mean a lot to him; more so since discussing the praying mantis creatures' map and the conspiracy speculation surrounding Truxxe. It made him feel strange to realise that he had feelings for an alien – particularly one who saw him as being naked when he wore his compsuit.

Payday eventually arrived and Tom lined up in Tyrander's office with his equally eager colleagues at the end of the shift on the seventh rotation. Tyrander gave the impression of being a headmaster allotting punishments to a line of disobedient children queuing at his desk, rather than a manager presenting well-earned pay cheques to his employees. But Tom didn't mind the air of superiority or the bellowing vocals today - he simply waited, grinning expectantly. On Tom's turn, the rotund Truxxian pushed a thick envelope into his hand, but when Tom went to pull his hand away Tyrander held it there. His bushy monobrow raised and his piggy eyes bore into him.

"Congratulations on completion of your first week, Mr. Bowler," he boomed. "You'll find your staff pass is in there too." Tom, taken aback, widened his grin.

"Thank you." Tom walked past the rest of the queue and waited for Raphyl in the staff room. He opened his envelope and found the payslip inside indicating how much he had earned. Tom laughed to himself at the situation. His first ever payslip and he was on a different planet – but how Earthly the concept seemed. He soon discovered that the set-up was more Earthly still when he noticed a tax deduction of 50d. He shrugged as he discovered that the number in the net income box was higher than he had expected at 200D, even after the fee for his lodgings had been deducted. He felt that having some money of his own would make his feel less dependent and less limited on this alien world. Raphyl soon joined him in the staff room, his grin twice as wide as Tom's.

"It's the best day of the week, Tombo."

"Even better for you, Raphyl, here's the money I owe you for the compsuit and the timepiece," Tom handed him a few sheets of the monopoly-esque printed paper. "And here's a few drink's worth I'm sure I owe you," he added, pushing yet more sheets into Raphyl's lean lilac hands.

"Thanks!" exclaimed Raphyl, and Tom was sure that if his friend's grin had been any wider then his face would split in two. "I suppose you want to go and redeem your session at the holoceiver place then?"

"You read my mind," Tom quipped. "But first... do you mind if we *don't* have the complimentary meal today? I've had enough ruffleberry milkshakes and "meat" burgers to last me a lifetime."

"OK Mr. Moneybags, where do you want to go?"

"Can you recommend anywhere?"

"OK, follow me." Raphyl deposited his well-earned denominations in the folds of his uniform. He led the way past many bustling outlets and eateries full of employees already undoubtedly enjoying payday. They passed the Holoceiver Exchange and soon arrived at a small cafeteria at the very end of one of the vast corridors. "Romey's," announced Raphyl. "Other than the free meal at work, this is the place I choose to eat." Tom could see why - the seating area was patently smaller than the restaurant where they both worked but the café didn't seem to suffer from over-crowding as did many of the places they had passed. The air was sweet with the smell of cooking; proper cooking, not the over-processed imported conveyor-belt food which Tom had found himself serving.

"They only serve home grown Truxxian food in here, and it has a bit more taste than the food at the express cuisine." Raphyl sank into a green ergonomic seat which shifted around him deferentially. Tom took the seat opposite him and looked around. He was impressed.

"How come you haven't shown me this place before?"
The reply came as a whisper. "Well, I kind of... er... I haven't paid my tab for a while. But we've been paid now so..."

Raphyl waved his newly acquired notes. As though the wad of bills had been a magnetic instrument, a robot waiter suddenly appeared at the table. Tom found it difficult not to laugh at its crudely painted on bow tie on its bronze body and the aloof manner in which it attempted to hold itself.

"Ah, Mr. Raphyl," a deep male voice emitted him from a grille on the robot's face. "It's about time you settled your bill with us."

"I'm surprised you didn't seize me on my way in through the door!" Raphyl laughed. "All right, here you go." He peeled a few sheets from his grasp and reluctantly handed them to the expectant waiter. "I'll have the usual." The automaton attendant gave a partial bow before turning to Tom. Tom bit his lip and tried not to laugh aloud. Was this how ridiculous Miss Lolah looked to those not under her pheromone spell? He was bewildered to think that he could be attracted to such a contraption. He found it hard to think straight.

"Err… yeah I'll just have the same," he said quickly, having not even considered the menu or asking what was on offer. The waiter performed another semi bow, turned and walked away, head held high. His gait was only a little less clumsy than that of Miss Lolah. Tom, unable to stop himself, gave a whimper of laughter. "I don't know why but I found him very amusing!"

"He's not so amusing when you owe him money I can tell you!" Raphyl said seriously. Tom decided not to ask details but continued to watch a replica waiter go about its duty elsewhere in the restaurant. Tom's face fell when he realised that one of the customers he was serving was Kayleesh. Who was she with? Tom strained to look around the waiter. They seemed to be taking a long time to order, whoever it was. When eventually the robot had bowed and left the table, Tom saw that she was dining with a praying mantis creature. And they seemed to be very close, leaning forwards and whispering to each other. Surely she wasn't attracted to *him?* Tom felt a burning seed of envy germinate inside him. Why had she gone sneaking out for a date with *him?* She could see every compsuit-wearing being on the station in their bare skin and she was having dinner with an *insect?* Surely she'd be more interested in someone… in someone like him? Tom felt betrayed by her.

"What are you scowling at?" Raphyl asked, clearly too lazy to turn around.

Tom looked at him. "Um, nothing." He decided to change the subject. "So, what is it I've ordered exactly?"

"Kwelps and hanaken sauce," Raphyl answered. A pointed purple tongue emerged for a moment and licked his thin lilac lips. Tom raised an eyebrow.

"And that is…?"

"Kwelps are shellfish - bred in Truxxe's oceanic farms. And the sauce just makes them taste even better. You'll love them."

Tom smiled politely. His stomach began to rumble. He hoped that his friend's recommendation was reliable. His focus slipped back to the couple behind Raphyl. Kayleesh and her date were still talking very closely. If only he could hear what they were saying. Perhaps it would be better if he didn't know – it would only anger him further. The waiter arrived at the table, distracting him from the devoted duo. He placed a plate in front of each of them. Next he positioned two small dishes in the middle of the table, which were brimming with a green substance. A dozen or so shells the size and colour of conkers occupied the plate. His stomach rumbled again. He really hoped that kwelps were to his taste. Not seeing any form of cutlery or any means of opening the shells he picked one up in his hands. He began to prise it open with his fingers as though he were opening a pistachio shell to retrieve the nut inside. It opened with surprising ease, but he recoiled as the thing began to snap and nip at his fingers in retort. Tom dropped the kwelp back onto the plate noisily and glared accusingly at Raphyl. Raphyl was grinning at him and holding his bowl of sauce in his hand.

"That's very brave, trying to eat a kwelp *without* the hanaken sauce."

"What do you mean?" Tom asked crossly, sucking his sore fingers.

"Watch." Tom watched as Raphyl arranged his meal so that there was a gap in the centre of a circle of kwelps. He gently poured the contents of the sauce bowl into the gap and set the bowl back down. Moments later, the shells nearest to the green sauce pool began to creak open and small, naked, pink, slug-like creatures began to emerge. They inched towards the sauce, allowing themselves to be submerged in the substance, bathing in it, their shells snapping shut behind them. The next row behind them must have sensed what was happening because they too surfaced from the safety of their shells and progressed to the green fluid. Tom watched, open-mouthed, both disgusted and fascinated. A mauve hand plucked one of the sauce-covered creatures between fore finger and thumb and plopped it into Raphyl's mouth.

"Self-preparing food. Perfect!"

"Was that still alive?" Tom's eyebrows were raised so high that they were almost vertical.

"Does it matter?" Raphyl asked, reaching for another.

"Well... I suppose not. Seeing as it's going to be eaten anyway..." Tom gulped, took a deep breath. He created a gap in the centre of his own plate with his fingers and poured in the sauce. The warm, thick sauce did smell appetising, he had to admit, despite its noxious-looking colouring. Sure enough, the kwelps willingly left the sanctuary of their individual casing and preceded willingly towards the lake of death. Tom felt a pang of guilt in the midst of his hunger pains. Once he was sure that one of them was fully submerged, Tom reached down and removed the dripping, naked kwelp. It felt like soft flesh, wriggling in his fingers. He closed his eyes and put it in his mouth before he could change his mind, careful to bring his teeth down on it as quickly as he could. He didn't like the thought of a live creature edging its way back up his throat. He chewed two or three times and then swallowed. The flavour wasn't like any seafood Tom had ever experienced. It tasted unexpectedly like pork. Pork in applesauce. He nodded and smiled to himself.

"Not bad," Tom confessed. Raphyl grinned back at him, sauce dripping from his chin. Tom finished the meal as quickly as he could; his speed driven by both hunger and the need to finish it before he could think too much about what he was putting in his mouth. Once his plate had been emptied of kwleps, and only a smear of sauce remained, Tom's attention returned to Kayleesh. She and the green being opposite her were eating a complicated looking meal with what looked to Tom like over-sized cutlery. Envy brewed inside him. He turned to Raphyl.

"Can we go?" he said rather curtly. Raphyl looked a little confused at his haste but didn't ask questions. He ran a long finger across his plate and licked off the green sauce with his purple tongue.

"You're keen to go to the holoceiver exchange aren't you Tombo? OK but I don't want to get in debt with this place again – we should wait for the waiter to bring the bill."

Tom and Raphyl made their way back down the passageway towards the Holoceiver Exchange. *She was probably too preoccupied with her date to even notice that we were there,* Tom thought. As they entered the shop, Tom remembered that the attendant communicated telepathically and so tried to push his feelings for Kayleesh aside in case his thoughts got him into trouble. He didn't want a total stranger knowing his innermost feelings.

# CHAPTER 17

They entered the pale green reception room. The row of doctor's waiting room style seats was occupied bar two. The yellow translucent, faceless bubble was bobbing up and down behind the low counter. Tom put his hand in his pocket, took the appointment slip and showed it to the creature which had excreted it two days earlier.

"I have an appointment. On the sixth hour," he said aloud.

"Please take a seat," the words were planted in his head.

Tom took a seat next to Raphyl who looked as though he had already made himself at home. Tom clutched the slip nervously. He wasn't sure why he was nervous. Perhaps it was the clinical tone of the room. He should have been excited about speaking to his parents, but he didn't know what he was going to say to them. He wished he had thought this through more. When Tom's turn eventually came, he made his way towards the door where the green holographic lettering now read "vacant".

"I'll wait here," Raphyl gave him a half-wave.

"OK." Tom nodded and went through the door. He found himself in a room a quarter of the size of the one he had just left - merely a booth. He didn't know what he had expected to find, but it certainly wasn't the scene he saw before him. He had imagined some kind of telephonic contraption at least, but instead all he saw was another translucent-yellow bubble. The being was much larger than the one in the reception room and stood a good six feet high in front of Tom. The bubble form was quivering like an over-sized party jelly and Tom was horrified to notice that this one was naked. Tom would have avoided looking the alien in the eye at this point, had it possessed any. He shifted uncomfortably on the spot and strained to look behind the creature, as he felt rather rude simply looking through him. However, there was nothing else in the room on which he could transfix his focus.

"Er... is this the right room for the holoceiver?"

"Yes, I am he," a voice iterated in genderless tones inside his mind.

"Excuse me?"

"I am the holoceiver. Please step inside so that we can connect your call."

"Step inside?" Tom spun around. The only door in the room was the one by which he had entered. "Inside where?"

"Please step inside," the almost mechanical, insipid voice repeated. Tom took a step back.

"I can sense that you are afraid. Do not be." Tom felt like opening the door and asking Raphyl what was going on, but he wanted to appear brave and stood his ground for now. He had to figure out some things on his own.

"I'm not afraid," Tom lied then flinched as he noticed that the bubble body was approaching him. It grew closer and closer and didn't stop when it was right up close to the human.

"Er... what are you -" his words were cut off as the great bubble pressed against him. He braced himself to feel crushed, but instead Tom realised that the bubble had pushed a through him so that he was now encased inside it. Too shocked to speak or even take a breath, Tom looked around him. The booth was tinged with yellow. He looked down at his body, which had been surrounded by this bubble-being suit. He felt sick. He was inside an alien. He pushed a hand against the inside of the viscous skin. Trapped. Suddenly, having seen the appointment slip materialise inside one of these things didn't seem half as strange as what was happening to him now. How was he going to get out?

"Where would you like to call?" the voice reverberated louder than ever inside his head. Tom realised that he had been holding his breath and his fingers were beginning to tingle from lack of oxygen. He flexed them. He said his address out loud, anxiety welling up inside him.

"Please do not fear me. I am the means through which the connection will take place. My telepathic force will carry your image to your required caller, and you will be able to communicate. It is perfectly safe. Please do not be alarmed. The connection will be made shortly." Tom wished that it would stop reassuring him; somehow this only made him feel worse. There was a gurgling, sucking sound like the rushing of water through a plughole. Tom's vision was momentarily blurred. He closed his eyes. The gurgling stopped and Tom opened his eyes slowly. He was standing outside his own front door back at home. He looked down at his body. It was no longer encased by the bubble, or so it seemed. He found that he was wearing dark jeans and a hooded top. He felt his pockets, hopefully, for a key and found that he had one. He turned it in his fingers.

*How convenient,* he smiled to himself. *It's like a dream.* Tom unlocked the front door.

"Hello?" he called along the hallway.

"We're up here, dear," he recognised his mother's voice, although it sounded a little croaky. Tom advanced up the stairs three at a time. "In the bedroom." Tom opened his parent's bedroom door slowly and found that they were both lying on top of the bed, a single blanket draped across them. Tom saw two half-full boxes of tissues on the bed, amongst discarded throat-sweet wrappers.

"Are you OK?" Tom asked, concerned.

"We're fine, dear," his mother croaked. "Just don't come any closer – I don't want you taking any germs back to that restaurant." Tom nodded and sat on a chair by the window.

"Are you sure you're alright?" Tom felt like he had abandoned his parents. He had never known both his parents to be ill at the same time.

"It's only the 'flu Tom. So, what have you been up to these past few days? Getting on all right?" His father's voice suggested that his nose was very bunged up. A proceeding series of sniffs reaffirmed this.

"Yes, yes I'm getting on well thanks. I've picked up the job quite quickly. Nothing to it really," Tom replied, a little distractedly.

"And your colleagues? Are they helping you settle in OK?" his mother wiped her nose with a fresh tissue.

"Yes, they're pretty easy to get on with. Made a couple of friends, you know." Tom tried to sound as casual as he could, not wanting to give away too much information.

"Did you come up here on your own?" his mother asked. "You didn't ask a friend to travel up with you for the ride?"

"Er..." Tom imagined how his family would react to the purple-skinned Raphyl, the pixie-faced Kayleesh or any member of Hasprin's Legion. He bit his lip, attempting not to laugh.

"He's not a child anymore, Fiona. He's quite capable of travelling on his own now," his father's saving words spilt out of his mouth. Tom nodded.

"I see enough of them at work," he grinned. "I do have some news though. I've joined a sort of... team. We play in the evenings."

"A team? Surely not football? You've never enjoyed your sport." Tom's father popped a throat sweet into his mouth and began sucking on it.

"No, not football. It's more of a... pub game."

"Pool? Skittles? Darts?"

"Yes... darts," Tom nodded.

"I see, well that's good," his father gave what Tom considered to be a smile of approval. "A bit more sociable than computer gaming, eh? You still play those space adventures, Tom?" he asked, jovially.

"No...not really. Real life is much more interesting."

"That's what I always, said," his mother agreed. "Now, would you like something to eat?"

Tom remembered that his form was merely a projection into this suburban home. He was so many light years away, yet here he was having a conversation with his parents as though he had never left them. Despite the encircling 'flu germs – from which he was thankfully safe – Tom felt comforted to be in his parent's presence, having missed them so much. He wished he could feel the heat of the room; smell the soothing aromas of eucalyptus and menthol cold treatments. "There was a buffet car on the train. I'll be all right for a while. If you two are OK I was going to go and see if I could find Max and Nathan." Tom stood up to leave. His mother nodded.

"That's a good idea. I'd rather you weren't exposed to these germs for too long and I know they've both missed you. Take care, now. And next time, call ahead!" She gave a feeble wave, accompanied by a nod of his father's head, followed by a sneeze into an already full tissue.

"See you both." Tom made his way down the stairs. He noticed on his descent that the stair which always creaked made no sound, as the pressure from his foot was not actually present. For a moment he wondered whether his parents had noticed this. Had they suspected anything strange about his appearance? Tom hoped that if they had then they would have thought their illness the reason, and their dulled senses. They wouldn't realise what had really happened. They couldn't. It wouldn't have occurred to them.

Reassuring himself, Tom exited the house and made his way to the street where Nathan lived. He was looking forward to seeing his friend again. Soon, he was approaching the familiar red painted wooden door he knew so well. One of the glass panes still wore a hairline crack like a badge of honour, where Nathan had accidentally slammed a tennis ball from the opposite side of the road more than ten years ago. He lifted his hand to knock; however, he was startled to find that his fist passed right through the red door. Then how come he had been able to unlock his own front door? He looked at his hands, at his feet. His tapped his toes. The paved driveway beneath them didn't seem as though it was properly supporting him. Was his presence here already fading? He hadn't been certain whether he would be able to touch things here, but he had been able to climb stairs, sit on chairs and push open his parent's bedroom door. He was considering his quandary when the front door opened.

"Hello, Tom!" Nathan's mother Carol exclaimed, wild green eyes scanning his face. She could see him, at least. "How is the new job? Nathan is in the front room with Max, go on through. Must dash!" Carol took a set of car keys from her pocket and unlocked the door to the people carrier, which was parked on the driveway. "Bye, now!" she called cheerily and started the engine, before reversing off the driveway and heading towards whatever engagement she was evidently late for. Tom smiled. Carol was always busy doing something or going somewhere. It was nice to see her again. He sidled through the open door and walked along the hallway and through the house, which was identical, in layout, to his own. He found Nathan and Max on the settee with game controllers in their hands, jerking left and right as their respective souped-up vehicles were speeding their way along a race-track on-screen. The volume on the television set was high; droning car engines, a cheering crowd and an up-beat backing track.

"Hey," Tom stepped in front of the screen and grinned.

"Hey, get out of the way of the - Tom!" Nathan dropped his controller in surprise.

Max pressed the pause button and the noise ceased. "You're back!"

"Yep… kind of… not for long though." Tom waved a hand through Nathan's – knowing that it would pass through. Nathan jumped, clearly stunned.

*"What?"*

"I'm not really here," Tom began to explain. "This is just a projection."

Nathan looked around. "A projection from what?"

"I'm not sure how it works, exactly. Well, I'm not sure how it works at all, but basically my body is in a neighbouring galaxy and this is the best way of communicating with you back here."

"Now *this* is some elaborate prank." Nathan stood up, his eyes were wide, his jaw, slack. He lunged forwards and punched the air where Tom's ribs should have been. Instead, his fist passed straight through, causing him to stumble from the lack of rebound. "Whoa."

"I told you, didn't I?" Max said smugly, grinning.

"Yeah, but I never thought… not really… this is *amazing*. So… have you really been working… up there? I mean…" Nathan was lost for words for the first time Tom could recall. This made him laugh. Max started laughing too.

"Yes, I've been serving burgers to aliens!" he exclaimed.

"Aliens eat *burgers?*"

"Yes. Everyone likes burgers."

"True. Any hot alien babes?" Nathan asked, cheekily.

"Yeah, kinda. There is one… although most of them are pretty weird looking!"

"Weird, how?" Max asked, taking a seat once more. Tom explained to his friend and cousin about the people he had encountered, the Spotoon team, the TSS building, the holoceiver creature. For the first time ever, he was having more of an adventure than Nathan. He was actually baffling and entertaining *him* with his stories. He had dreamed of this day.

"I'm inside an alien now," Tom divulged, almost smugly. "Well, my body on Truxxe is, at least. That's how the holoceiver works. It's like a large bubble you step inside which speaks through your mind." He gesticulated as he explained.

"Is it speaking to you now?" Nathan asked, eyes wide.

"No, not now. I don't know what it's doing now. Just… harbouring my body, I guess."

"Gross, bud." Max made a face.

"Awesome," grinned Nathan.

"So what's been happening here? Anything… uh oh…"

"What?" Nathan's face dropped. Tom looked at the two of them through a continually yellowing glaze. He was beginning to feel detached. And then he did hear his "host" speaking to him. The androgynous voice echoed around his mind and inside his bubble cage.

"Your time has elapsed. Please prepare for disconnection."

"Er… I think I've got to go, guys," Tom looked down and saw that his feet were no longer in contact with the carpeted living room floor, merely floating an inch or so above it. He looked up. Nathan and Max looked confused.

"Can you still see me?"

"You still seem to be here," Nathan replied. He waved a hand through his friend again, unnecessarily. "Kind of…"

"Well, I'll come back and say hi again soon… if I can afford it," he added. "Remember – not a word to my parents of the… weirdness. Have a pint for me at the local!" Tom said rather loudly, for he was afraid that he was fading. Through the darkening yellow veil, Tom could just make out two perplexed faces. He blinked and when he opened his eyes, his vision was blurred, and the gurgling and sucking sounds filled his ears. His consciousness had returned to the holoceiver room on planet Truxxe.

Hannond Putt saw that the holoceiver sign had morphed to *vacant* and stood up, expectantly. The door opened and a disorientated-looking human emerged. Hannond recognised him from the Spotoon game against Hasprin's Legion, but there were more pressing matters at hand than conversing with the opposition. He knew he had to report back to Schlomm. Not because he missed his brother, but because he knew that Schlomm had the patience of a young Glorbian waiting in a queue for a Burnberry Ice Cream on a stick on a hot day on Glorb.

"Greetings, Schlomm," proclaimed Hannond as his sibling came into view through the fading, yellow haze. He saw that his sudden manifestation had startled his brother.

"AH!" Scholmm took a step back; his hand flew to his mature heart, which was situated in the lower right-hand side of his body. "Don't *do* that to me!"

"Sorry," Hannond said, with utter sincerity.

"So… any news?" The elderly Glorbian made an attempt to compose himself. The grey being padded his way to a low seat in the Cluock spacecraft, eyes fixed on Hannond's projection.

"I joined a Spotoon team!" Hannond announced, animatedly.

"You've what?" Schlomm boomed. "I sent you to do a job, Hannond. Here I am, parked on a Pus-awful planet at the opposite end of the galaxy, waiting for news of our plot, and you tell me you've joined a *Spotoon team*. You're *making friends!*" he said thickly. "Never mind, I suppose it helps to support your cover as a regular employee."

"That's what I thought," Hannond agreed, quickly.

"Hmm," Schlomm gave the impression that he wasn't entirely convinced. "So, exactly how much progress have you made?" he tapped his sagging, coarsely haired chin with his thick fingers, in anticipation.

"I've managed to secure a position in the sewage preliminary filter zone," Hannond announced, attempting to persuade his brother into thinking that this had been a particularly challenging stage of the plan. But Schlomm's brain dismissed subtleties. Cold hard facts were what his schemes craved. Schlomm's expression was unchanging. So Hannond continued. "There's no sign of the gems yet, but I don't think it'll be long now. I have heard that the batch you delivered is in circulation so it shouldn't be long…"

"…before the digestive juices work their magic," finished Schlomm. A grin spread across his hoary face. Schlomm dropped to the ground and waddled over to his brother. Before he could speak, Hannond instinctively took a step backwards and said, "There may be… a… *small* problem though." Schlomm's face dropped so far his already wilting chin merged with his chest. "It's… it's just that I am assigned to work alongside a… Strellion. And as you know, they're a notoriously inquisitive race." To his surprise, Schlomm's grin crept back across his face.

"A *Strellion,* you say? Hmm…" Schlomm tapped his fingers on his chin once more in thought. "You are right – they are a *meddlesome* people by nature, but they are also legendary for their accumulative skills." If Hannond had had any eyebrows he would have involuntarily raised one at this point.

"And that means…?" Hannond ventured. Schlomm pulled himself up to his full, but arguably short, height.

"It *means,* Hannond, that they are able to hoard items about their body – the way the land hamster-mole stores its food inside its great cheeks for later consumption." A glimmer of iniquity flashed across his face. Hannond could almost hear his brain plotting away underneath that thick-skinned skull. "You thought that the great white mass of a Strellion was body fat?

Oh no, it most likely contains whatever's on the menu for the next five rotations."

"I wondered why he doesn't come to the Express Cuisine with the rest of the workers at lunchtime," Hannond said, half to himself.

"Hannond, my boy, I think you have discovered the key to the secondary stage of the transit of the gems!"

# CHAPTER 18

"Was it worth the wait then?" Raphyl dipped his long, lilac tongue into the brown liquid with which was his customary drink.

"Yes… yes it was… strange. I don't know what feels more unreal – going back home in that manner or coming back *here*."

Raphyl shrugged. "I don't understand you sometimes, Tombo."

Six Seven was busier than usual. Tom presumed this was on account of the fact that it was payday. Raphyl looked up from his drink.

"Hey, look, there's Kayleesh, over at the bar," Raphyl observed. Tom's heart leapt and then plummeted as he envisioned her dining with the praying mantis creature. He forced himself not to look up and instead pretended that there was something interesting floating in the head of his beer. He prodded at the non-existent article with his finger, attempting to look indifferent. *Don't call her over,* he pleaded, silently. But it was too late. She had seen them.

"Hi," Kayleesh sat in the seat next to Tom and set her drink on the table. Tom could smell her captivating fragrance, fused with the potent contents of her glass. He hated himself for feeling the way he did about her. Nothing could come of it. She obviously preferred the company of a creepy-crawly. Perhaps they had come here to finish their date. Tom looked up but there was no sign of the green, leggy character.

"Hi Tom, everything all right?" Kayleesh beamed at him, her golden hair gleaming in the softly lit room.

Tom made a minimal response, "Uh huh." Kayleesh took a single swallow of her thin drink before it escaped entirely in a gaseous form from her glass.

"You two won't believe this," she looked at them both, wide-eyed. She looked as though she was about to burst. "I've been talking to someone," she began. Tom took his attention back to his glass and narrowed his eyes. "His name is Hyganty. He's a conspiracy theorist. He knows about the map. He was the one who wrote it." Tom looked up.

"Is that… that green praying mantis you were talking to?" Tom looked up, suddenly interested.

"The green what?" Kayleesh had evidently no knowledge of this Earthly insect. "He's a Submian, and yes, he's green," she said simply. "Not that it matters. Anyway, he has another copy of that map – with similar annotations. One which doesn't reek of ruffleberry milkshake." She threw Tom a sideways glance. Tom's eyes scanned the table and flickered to the Augtopian's empty hands.

"Well, where is it?"

"The map? Oh, Hyganty still has it. But the point is that he is convinced that there is more to the existence of this planet than pure luck."

"Here we go again…" Raphyl rolled his eyes and leaned back in his chair, dismissively. He folded his arms - a figurative barrier from the conversation. Kayleesh shook her head and her intent gaze felt on Tom.

"The Submians believe that this place is no accident."

"I gathered that from the map we saw. They suppose that the planet was created to profit from fuel and… burger sales."

"Not… exactly," Kayleesh leaned forwards and a strand of her golden hair fell in the path of her sticky tripedal glass. Tom's eyes glanced back at her elfin face. What had she discovered? "The Submians believe that this industry," she waved her hands in a general manner at this point, looking about the room, "was not the *reason* for the creation of the planet but a *bi-product* of something else… rather, serendipitous." Tom furrowed his brow.

"So, the mining and the whole service industry here is just a *happy accident* from something much bigger?"

"Exactly," a smile spread across her face.

"Right… so… what are the Submians doing here?"

"Have you no sense of adventure?" Kayleesh sat up. Tom's expression grew to one of further confusion.

"Obviously I have, or I wouldn't be here!" he took a long pull from his glass and wiped a drip from his chin. Kayleesh looked at him quizzically as though she didn't consider an evening spent in a bar on an alien planet an adventure.

"They're here and in the neighbouring galaxies gathering *evidence*."

"Oh, so they're like detectives?"

"Well, more like conspiracy theorists with some gumption. Anyway, I'm going with them."

"Going with them where?" Tom still wasn't comfortable with the idea of her spending so much time in the company of someone other than himself.

"To explore, to gather evidence – don't you want to find out about the planet we live and work on?" She said, excitedly. More adventure? Could Tom's brain cope with further input of otherworldly concepts? Would it be dangerous?

"I'll come along," Raphyl said, almost inaudibly. He sat forward in his chair once more and took a casual mouthful of his Truxxian Gloop. "Just for a laugh, you understand. I don't care about the intent of your little quest, particularly."

"Well it's a start." Kayleesh beamed at him.

"Er… me too," Tom agreed before he could stop himself. "So when is this little expedition?"

"Tomorrow. I'm meeting Hyganty and the others in the dock at the tenth hour. So we'll need a good night's sleep."

"The dock? We're going in a spaceship?" Tom asked, suddenly feeling as nervous as he had on the day he had left Earth.

"Of course," Kayleesh stood up to depart.

"Kayleesh," he called after her. "We won't be in the way will we… of you and Hyganty?" Kayleesh laughed genuinely and flicked back her fair mane.

"What are you talking about, Tom?" Kayleesh left the bar and Tom remained in his seat, with a huge grin on his face.

A rapid knocking broke Tom's dream.

"You ready, Tom?" came Kayleesh's excited voice through his apartment door. Tom mumbled a sleepy reply. The artificial environment hadn't yet progressed along its programme to daylight. The room was bathed in a sallow light, with barely enough strength for Tom to be able to make out the basic shapes of his sparsely furnished apartment. Yawning, he managed to locate and don his compsuit. He splashed his face with cold water, brushed his teeth and seized a fruit bar snack from his pocket. He emerged from his apartment, chewing slowly on the fruit bar. A weary-looking Raphyl was standing behind the eager Kayleesh. She looked so excited that Tom thought she was about to take off. Raphyl and Tom yawned in unison.

"Come on then." Tom managed a smile at his friends. The three of them made their way to the spaceport. They walked across the alabaster white tiles of the huge foyer. The high-walled vestibule soon gave way to the vast openness of the spaceport. Tom was as amazed by enormity of the place as he had been on his arrival. An infinite array of diverse crafts, hefty as battleships or delicate as spider webs, occupied the floor space. Kayleesh appeared to know towards which one they were heading so he and Raphyl followed in her wake, Tom constantly craning his neck to take in the sheer beauty and size of some of the ships. Raphyl, however, sauntered along, scruffy, hands in his pockets, head bowed, with his eyes half-closed.

Tom was glad that Kayleesh had invited them. Working in the Express Cuisine the past few days had made him lose some perspective of the wonder of his situation. He really needed the opportunity to come out of his comfort zone again. Kayleesh stopped – so suddenly in fact that Tom, eyes fixed some thirty metres above them, walked straight into her.

"Sorry," he said.

"This is a Submian ship," she announced, gleefully. "Impressive, isn't it?" Tom looked up at the military-green craft before them. It was indeed, impressive. The core of the ship was the size of a multi-storey car park, made from robust looking material welded together with bolts the width of tree stumps. High above their heads, horned protrusions jutted out, painted in the same cargo green. The ship looked as though it would withstand a nuclear attack. A ramp led up to a hardy-looking door, which was beginning to open. Hyganty appeared and greeted the three travellers with a wave. They made their way up the ramp and climbed aboard. Once inside, they passed through a huge metal-lined corridor, their shoes ringing on the hard military floor as they walked. The decor of the corridor complemented the exterior design of the ship. Hyganty leading the way, they eventually reached a contrastingly comfortable-looking passenger suite. Eight lavish low-rise chairs equipped with intellibelts ran around the perimeter of the room. A visual display unit on one of the walls showed the outside view, so Tom, Raphyl and Kayleesh chose seats opposite it and the intellibelts snaked their way across their laps. *Much more comfortable than the TSS transit,* Tom observed as he relaxed into the seat. *And more supportive on the old back than an ergonomic chair.* Hyganty remained standing in the doorway.

"We're going to survey a planet on the far side of this galaxy," he informed them, his mandibles twitching. "A planet called Hushgah. We hope to arrive on about the second hour. I'll bring you some refreshments once we're safely on course." He turned and left, the door sleeking shut behind him.

Tom's eyes were fixed on the visual display unit on the opposite wall. He was aware that he had not yet consciously experienced an entire space flight, and there had been no window or viewing screen in his sleeping quarters aboard the TSS transit ship on this journey to Truxxe. On departing from the brightly lit port, the cumbersome craft accelerated almost without warning through the dark sky, soaring at a colossal speed. Tom felt as though he had been pasted onto his seat, his face locked in a traumatized contortion, his fingernails rooted into the arms of the luxury flight seat. His view of the VDU was a mere blur such was the intense momentum of the ascent. All of the coloured mixed into one; green, black, purple and a kind of flashing orange. He felt as though his eyes were crying tears of blood from the intense compression. *How long is this going to last?* He asked himself. Of course, he had not experienced the 10G take off when he had left the Earth. The Truxxian ship had made its brief, ephemeral journey to the edge of space almost unnoticed. How Tom wished that this crude craft could adopt that technique. Just as Tom was thinking he'd never be able to take a full lungful of air again, the acceleration began to decrease. He looked around him, speechless, his hand on his chest. Raphyl looked unfazed, in fact Tom realised that his friend was actually grinning. Kayleesh, between them, looked somewhat flustered, but after several deep breaths, she appeared to be recovering rather rapidly.

"That was fun," Raphyl exclaimed loudly.

"No it wasn't," Kayleesh said crossly. She had almost composed herself fully, now. "Are you OK, Tom?" She asked, kindly.

"Yes... yes I'm OK," Tom breathed and forced a smile, a little embarrassed. He blinked several times and focused his attention on the VDU; the stars sheer streaks of white across the obscurity of space. He didn't want to think about what kind of speed they were travelling. He swallowed, feeling a little nauseated. Raphyl was still grinning, maniacally.

"This must be one of the few ships left to power its initial take off by rocket fuel," he spouted, with more enthusiasm than Tom had ever heard emitted from Raphyl's mouth. The excitement in his face was comical; a child's first ride on a roller coaster. "I've heard of these still existing, but I never thought I'd ever get to travel in one – and I've flown in loads of ships. This is so much more interesting."

"So, what's moving us now that we're airborne? It must be something far more advanced for us to be travelling so far," Tom pointed at the VDU, his hand still a little shaky from the experience.

"Some kind of space warping drive I expect," he informed him, dismissively, before passionately adding, "I can't wait until we take off again!" The door to their suite shushed open. Hyganty strode into the room on his green, insectile legs. Tom was startled to discover that his attire had changed dramatically from the comp-suit illusion which had been projected whilst in the confines of the TSS complex. Instead of the vision of casual clothing to which Tom had become accustomed, the xenomorph was clad in what he would only describe as skin-tight semi-transparent leggings and a military-green halter neck. Tom stifled a laugh and looked away from the creature who looked as though he had come in to ask directions to the nearest gay bar. Tom saw then that Raphyl was wearing what looked like patchwork trousers made from sections of many materials which Tom didn't recognise. His arms were wrapped in the same material and his lilac chest was bare. Kayleesh was wearing her TSS uniform, much to Tom's disappointment. Hyganty approached them, plastic-fibred trousers squeaking as he walked. Tom saw that Hyganty was carrying a rugged-looking holdall in one of his pincers. He dropped it to the floor with a thunk.

"Glow rocks – for the portable ALSID light bot," he said. "They'll come in handy as they don't occur naturally on the planet Hushgah. Of course, what we're on this mission to discover is – *do* they occur naturally on Truxxe?" he asked, rhetorically and turned to leave.

"Thanks, Hyganty," Kayleesh called after him. Hyganty raised a feeler as he exited, acknowledging her gratitude. Tom shivered. He still felt uneasy about the Submians, although he wasn't sure why. He didn't quite trust them yet. He stared hard at the VDU. The striking brilliant light of the stars appeared static as they tore past, occasional shapes blinking in and out of sight, which Tom assumed to be planets or asteroids.

"We only have rocket-powered shuttles on Earth," Tom informed them.

"You have them on Earth?" Raphyl's eyes widened. "So you've been on them a few times?"

"Not personally, no."

"Oh." Raphyl looked confused, almost disappointed.

Sometime later the craft began to decelerate, thrusters fighting against gravity as the rugged beast of a spaceship prepared to land. Tom squinted in involuntary protest. Presently, Hyganty and another identically clad Submian entered the room where Tom, Raphyl and Kayleesh were waiting, expectantly. Tom hoped that his amusement at the sight of the two of them together, dressed as they were, didn't show. The intellibelts slid compliantly back into their housing, allowing the three of them to rise. The other Submian was trailing two ALSID bots, the leash of one of which he handed to Kayleesh. She took it eagerly.

"Let's go!"

"Er… where are we going, exactly?" Tom asked.

"We're first going to meet up with some fellow conspiracy theorists," Hyganty gesticulated, meaning the two of them. "Meanwhile, if the three of you could go and explore – find out anything you can – that would help the movement." Tom wasn't sure if they could do a lot, wandering around on an alien planet, not knowing what they were supposed to be looking for exactly. "And we'll meet up later and discuss our findings," Hyganty blinked his vertical eyelids and somehow his mandibles gave the suggestion of a smile. Neither Kayleesh nor Raphyl made any signs of protest so he shrugged, resignedly. He didn't come all this way to sit through a meeting anyway. He decided that he would much rather be out exploring – evidence or no evidence. The two Submians and the TSS employees disembarked the ship. Tom was the last one to descend the ramp, eyes wide, taking in the new environment. They were outside. It was daylight. The ground beneath their feet was concrete – a wide pathway which paved the way to a large municipal-looking building.

"We'll be on the seventh floor if you need us. Otherwise we'll meet back here before sunset," said Hyganty, pointing a feeler in the direction of the building. The three of them nodded and Kayleesh stepped off the walkway and started in the opposite direction, ALSID bot in tow. Raphyl looked back at the ship, a look of yearning in his eyes. He was evidently pining for another adrenaline rush from the rocket-boosted craft.

"Come on, you. Let's get going," Kayleesh called. Tom and Raphyl looked at the path ahead of them, a dusty, barren landscape. Occasionally, a strange variety of tree could be seen dotted along the terrain, with dark branches, twisted around thick trunks. The foliage a pale green, waving in the moderate wind.

"Not much going on here," observed Raphyl.

"You never know," said Kayleesh. They walked several hundred yards, the warmth of the pale yellow sun on their backs. As they progressed, the wind began to pick up, lifting the dirt and whipping it around their feet. The dust began to rise as the force of the wind elevated and Tom folded his arms around his torso, bracing himself against it. He shielded his face with one arm and quickened his pace to keep up with Kayleesh and the ALSID bot.

"How can you see where we're going?" Tom called out to Kayleesh against the sound of the rushing air stream. But the din the wind was creating must have been too loud for her to hear him because there was no reply. Tom looked up, squinting, feeling as though his face was being bombarded with thousands of tiny needles. *"Kayleesh?"* But all Tom could see was an influx of dust and debris, heading in his direction, the wind forcing him to stumble backwards. He reached out behind him to bolster his fall and his grip met the twisted form of a tree. He brought his other hand around and held onto the trunk, feeling that if he let go he would blow away. He called out to his friends, but he couldn't even hear his own voice against the gale. What had happened? Where had this wind come from so suddenly? Where were they? They could have been feet away from him and Tom wouldn't have known it, such was the thick debris stew of the environment. Blinded by the dust, tears streaming down his face, he dug his nails into the bark for dear life. He was aware of a bright, flashing yellow light, which pulsated half a dozen times. Where was it coming from? Fruitlessly he continued to call out. He called out to Kayleesh, Raphyl, Hyganty. But all he could hear and all he could feel was the force of the wind. He hung there for what seemed like hours, screaming out, unable to release the tree or rest. Slowly, eventually, Tom was aware that the dust and debris was beginning to settle, the wind was dropping, and he was able to sustain his balance. Cautiously, he opened his stinging eyes and blinked, moisture blocking his vision. He realised that it had gotten dark. Tom slackened his grip, moved one hand and then the other. His hands were shaking from having held on so tightly and he could feel indentations from the bark embedded in his fingertips.

"Raphyl? Kayleesh?" He could hear his own voice now, the wind a mere breeze. But still there came no reply. Suddenly, Tom felt the ground beneath his feet begin to crumble and give way. Grabbing at the trunk once more for purchase, the rough trunk tore into his flesh as he fell helplessly into darkness.

# CHAPTER 19

Tom landed on his knees with a bump onto soft, mossy ground. His hands were sore and bloody, and the wet undergrowth cooled them. He looked up. He had fallen a good three metres. He was amazed that he hadn't been more badly hurt, despite the relatively soft landing. He stumbled to his feet, reaching out for something to stabilise him. In the darkness he felt his surroundings. He appeared to be in a pit some ten feet wide. He grappled around the perimeter wall - perhaps he could climb out, making use of tree roots and foot holes. To his consternation, but his fingers met walls slippery with moss. How was he going to get out? He called out the names of his friends once more, only to be answered by the echo of his own words. Echo? Tom realised that there must part of this underground place in which he'd found himself where the walls were hard and solid, allowing his voice to reverberate, where his words were not absorbed by moss. His eyes adjusting a little to the darkness now, Tom headed carefully across the slippery carpet towards what looked like a shadow in the wall - an opening perhaps? Arms outstretched, his hands touched nothingness as he progressed through a low archway. A sloping tunnel several metres long opened out into a much larger cavity. Tom stepped out into what resulted in being a great cavern, at least a hundred metres across. He looked up once more. The sides of the hollow here were higher still. Above him he could see that the churned-up remnants of the sandstorm were still clearing, and pinpoints of light were slowly making their presence known through the haze, *stars*. Desperate to return to the surface and be reunited with his friends, Tom began to climb the rocky wall, pulling himself up onto a narrow ledge and searching for foot holes. He made good progress, despite sometimes having to double-back if he could find no purchase in his chosen path. His heart was racing, his hands were sore, and his muscles ached from his fall, but pure adrenalin sped him on until

*What was that noise?* In surprise, Tom lost his grip and he began to plummet. His body bounced off the craggy wall and the hard ground came up to meet him.

Hannond had a sly look in his eye. He was pretending that he was trying to act secretly, although he knew that his actions were perfectly visible. And this is how he wanted it, for he hoped to arouse just enough suspicion from his colleague without having to be too obvious. He looked around him, which was no easy feat for a creature who nature had seemingly forgotten to bestow a proper neck. Consequently, his squat body bumbled left then right, his flat feet slapping on the warm wetness of the sewer floor as he turned. Hannond reached down into dark waters, not even grimacing at the odour or the texture between his fingers. Soon a look of pure delight spread across his face as his hand came into contact with something cool and hard. A refraction of orange light glimmered in his blue eyes. The Glorbian gem fit perfectly in the palm of Hannond's stubby hand. His smile of triumph widened as he felt the now-familiar warmth of the breath of a large, downy, dirty-white nose hover above his head. The great nostrils sniffed in their customary manner.

"Is that a crystal?" Eto's low voice contained a suggestion of wonder and excitement. It was time for Hannond to put the best of his acting abilities into play. He clamped one hand over the other, thus pretending to conceal the gem. He kept his back to the Strellion.

"Oh, Eto. I… I didn't see you there," he stammered slyly.

"What have you got? Can I see?" asked the curious creature.

"What do you mean? I haven't got anything."

"Yes you have, I saw it - in your hand. What is it, Hannond?" he asked in a manner which was enthusiastic but never threatening.

"It's… it's nothing." Hannond turned to his colleague and now held both hands behind his back, gem clasped tightly.

"Yes it is…you're holding it behind your back. Oh *please* Hannond – I won't tell anyone," begged Eto. Hannond looked around him in an obvious manner, continuing his performance. He appeared to give in.

"Oh, all right, but you mustn't tell anyone."

"I swear on my own spit-wielding saliva glands," said his fellow Spotoon team member in serious tones. Hannond brought his hands to the front of his body and slowly revealed the sparkling orange gemstone. The astonishment was apparent in Eto's face. *"Where did you get that from?"*

"Hush your tones, Eto. I don't want anyone to hear us," Hannond warned. "I found it – in this particular area amid the sewage." Eto's eyes widened.

"Do you suppose there could be *more* down there?" His speech had dulled to a whisper.

"Perhaps." Hannond saw Eto's eager gaze turn to the brown murkiness of the filtering cesspool. Without another word he proceeded to wade into the filth and feel around with greedy hands. Hannond was grateful that this taller and stronger creature was able to reach the areas he couldn't. He was turning out to be the perfect tool. After his gruelling time of labour in these pools, Hannond was now beginning to feel the excitement of the venture, his thoughts becoming more like those of his malevolent brother.

"There are many gems down here, Hannond!" a now brown Eto said, trying his hardest not to talk above a loud whisper. "I wonder how they got here."

"I don't know," lied Hannond. "Perhaps they were here all along. Now bring them up here before anyone sees you and we'll think of way to get them out unnoticed." Eto obediently came ashore, arms full of orange crystals. The proportions of the gems appeared to range from the smallness of a cherry to a large grapefruit, perhaps dependable on the size of the being which had excreted it. The Strellion gleefully stood in front of the Glorbian. He spoke the words which Hannond had been waiting to hear.

"I know of a way we can smuggle these out of here."

Once he had gained consciousness, Tom put his left hand to his head. Where was he? What was flashing? It seemed to be reflecting off the ground beneath him; its luminosity amplified. There was that noise again, louder this time. It sounded like a distorted digital alarm clock. He took his hand away from his face, pushed himself up to a sitting position. The noise was marginally quieter, the flashing, slightly muted. He found it difficult to think straight - his thoughts were muddled. Memories of being rudely roused from sleep by his alarm clock at home came back to him. The snooze button would be pressed half a dozen times before he managed to emerge from the comfort of his warm bed on a cold, dark, autumnal morning before making his journey to school. Here, in this alien ravine, instinct made him want to stop the noise.

"What am I doing here?" he said, out loud. It was then that Tom realised that the noise was coming from his wrist, the timepiece. And so was the pulsating yellow light. In confusion, wincing against the high-pitched tone, he took a closer look at the timepiece. He searched the clock face for a button or switch. In frustration and annoyance, Tom brought his fist onto the flat surface of the flashing timepiece. To his utter relief, the warped bleeping ceased, as did the flashing. *First time for everything – violence did actually help.* What were those symbols which had appeared on the clock face? He realised that he could no longer understand the timepiece in the absence of an ALSID unit. "Useless," he said out loud, although Tom couldn't have been more wrong.

"Tom!" Tom spun round. It was Kayleesh's voice.

"Where are you?"

"Here, Tom. Speak into your timepiece." Tom looked at his wrist once more.

"You're... how did you... what?" he spluttered. "You didn't tell me this freaky watch was also a... Where *are* you?"

"Where are *you* Tom?" It was so good to hear her voice once more. He was no longer alone. "We received your distress signal and began to follow it but then you stopped it."

"Distress signal? I'm... I'm at the bottom of a kind of chasm." Tom explained, looking around him. "More like a... a crater I suppose." Tom heard hushed voices. "I can't hear you," Tom said to his wrist.

"Look, if you want us to be able to find you, you'll need to set off your distress beacon again," came Raphyl's voice.

"Er... how do I do that?"

"The same way you set it off in the first place."

"Which was...?"

He could imagine Raphyl rolling his eyes at Tom's lack of relevant knowledge at this point.

"You need to get your heart rate at 80% of its maximum," Kayleesh said, patiently. "In other words – panic or run round a bit. Just until we get to you. Our own timepieces will lead us to you." Tom got to his feet, slowly.

"Well I can't run very fast... I hurt my ankle when I fell," Tom grimaced in pain. He also noticed that his shins and elbows were bleeding.

"Well you may need to – there are some big beasts who make their homes in craters in this part of the country," Kayleesh said firmly.

"There are *what?*" Suddenly, Tom's timepiece burst into life, flashing and beeping tremendously. *Well that worked,* thought Tom.

"Could there really be beasts down here or did you just say that to make me panic?" Tom shouted, but the alarm was too loud for him to make out any response. He didn't want to take any chances. Limping, he made his way to the tunnel mouth that led to the mossy pit into which he had fallen. His heart was racing sufficiently enough for the distress signal to continue sounding out. When his steps met the spongy under-footing, all Tom wanted to do was lie down and rest. He was emotionally exhausted. But he knew that if he did, then he would never be found or worse: he'd be eaten in his sleep. He circled the perimeter of the pit, ankle throbbing, fear of the potential "beast" spurring him on, feeding him adrenalin. He wasn't sure how many times his footsteps had circled the bottom of the pit, but eventually he heard familiar voices.

"Raphyl?" Tom looked up, breathless, shouting above the screaming watch. A lilac-complexioned face appeared over the rim of the trench.

"What you doing down there?"

"Just doing a bit of sightseeing," Tom quipped. "How am I going to get out?"

"You're not," said Kayleesh. "We're coming in."

"What? But why? Then we'll all be stuck down here," Tom protested.

"Who said that you're stuck? We're here finding evidence aren't we?"

"Yes."

"Well, you've found the biggest piece of evidence, Tom. Well done. Here, grab the ALSID bot." Tom took the weight of the heavy mechanism as Kayleesh and Raphyl lowered it towards him. He dropped the bulky bot to the ground as soon as he felt it was safe and before his arms broke off from the strain.

"What do you mean?" Tom asked. Next, a petite foot descended towards him. Tom obligingly guided the foot until Kayleesh was safely on the ground. They moved out of the way just in time to avoid Raphyl's unexpected sudden landing as he appeared next to them, grinning. "What happened anyway? Where did that freak weather come from?" Tom asked, limping behind Kayleesh as she strode towards the tunnel to the large, rocky cavern.

"Sandstorms aren't that freakish here on Hushgah apparently, Pretty common according to Hyganty,"

"Well why didn't he tell us?" Tom was concerned that his timepiece alarm would be activated again and took a few breaths to calm himself. "So, are there any 'crater beasts' then?" he asked Kayleesh.

"No – not on this planet anyway. In fact, this is the only crater on the whole planet. And you found it!"

"Lucky me," mumbled Tom.

"Bit of an anomaly in fact. Hyganty and the other conspiracy theorists have found similar phenomena on nine other planets – he mentioned it in the restaurant yesterday. That's why I thought we should take a look," Kayleesh turned back and smiled at him. That smile nullified any jealousy spasms which Tom felt at the sound of Hyganty's name.

"With a brain like yours, remind me why you work in an Express Cuisine again?" said Raphyl. Kayleesh giggled and shrugged.

"So there are other craters *like this* on other planets in the vicinity?" Tom was trying to follow her thread. "I don't understand what this has to do with Truxxe?"

"The craters haven't been on neighbouring planets, Tom. That's the point." Tom was even more confused, the pain from his leg sapping most of his concentration. Kayleesh did not elaborate at this point. She was more intent on examining the crater through which they were walking. Kayleesh suddenly stopped dead and looked down at the floor. "Have you noticed anything strange about the floor in here, Tom?"

"I know it hurt when I fell onto it!" Tom replied. He looked by his feet. It was then that he realised why the flashing light from his timepiece had looked as though it was reflecting in the floor. "Glass – there's glass on the floor. Something made of glass must have broken here. Something very large!"

"Nothing was *broken* – something was *formed,*" came a voice way above them. The voice echoed around the cavern. They looked up to see the green shape of Hyganty, high up on the ridge of the crater. The Submian bent his thin legs low until he was almost squatting on the floor. Unexpectedly, he then leapt

- higher than the mouth of the crater before landing gracefully on the ground next to Raphyl. Unscathed and completely composed, he reached a green pincer down to the ground and ran it across the rough compound.

*Why does everyone else* want *to be down here?* Tom thought as he rubbed soothingly at the wounds on his elbows. If the glass had been in shards rather than rough, compressed clumps he was certain that the gashes would have been more severe.

"This glass was once *sand,*" Hyganty continued. "It has been subjected to such an intense period of heat that it has become compressed."

"Well what's caused this amount of heat?" Kayleesh asked.

"That's what we need to find out."

On the edge of his vision, Tom noticed something shiny unravelling elegantly down the rocky wall. It was a ladder, fashioned from what appeared to be some kind of flexible metallic fabric. A second green figure peered over the rim of the cavern. He made a gesture with his pincers and feelers which Tom couldn't decipher. He was obviously out of the ALSID bot's range. Tom made a guess, however, that they were being beckoned and from Hyganty's reaction he was correct as he watched the Submian climb nimbly up the ladder, ALSID bot under his arm.

"Good old Frarkk!" he heard Hyganty exclaim ahead of him. Even with this burden he made light work of the ascent. Kayleesh, Raphyl and Tom followed. His leg throbbing, Tom pulled himself up onto the sandy ground where the others stood. He stood a while, massaging his foot.

"Hurt yourself, Tombo?" Raphyl asked as though it was the first time he had noticed he was even there. Tom nodded. "You should have said. I've got a fastac." Raphyl plunged his hand into the pocket of his peculiar trousers and took out what looked like a roll of sweets. "Fast acting pain relief," he said in reply to Tom's blank look. Tom took a tablet from the pack and swallowed it. His pain instantly diminished.

"That was pretty fast acting! Why didn't you tell me about these before, when I was in the medical room? That horrible headache lasted all day!" Tom asked, grimacing at the bitter flavour. Raphyl shrugged.

"I forgot they were in my pocket." Tom was too relieved to argue and, now that he was no longer distracted with the pain, pressed on with his questions as they walked back across the sandy, barren landscape.

"So what do we do next?"

"There's one more planet we need to visit – it has a crater like this one…" began Frarkk.

"What can it tell us that we haven't learned here? Or that anyone has discovered from the other craters?" asked Kayleesh…

"There is talk of some kind of machine – near the crater's edge."

"I think I'm still missing something here – what's the connection with these craters and Truxxe? Does Truxxe have a crater like this one too?" Tom asked.

"No. In fact the opposite is true – Truxxe is made up of many different materials, you understand?"

"Yes," said Kayleesh.

"Hence its appeal. However, the amount of landmass apparently absent from this and the other planets is equal to the mixed terrain which exists on Truxxe."

"You're saying that Truxxe is made up of these planets?" Kayleesh asked, excitedly.

"Perhaps. What we do know is that the South is original soil – the *true* Truxxe, if you like, and the rest…the rest came afterwards. We need to find out how. And why." There was something about Raphyl's continued silence which troubled Tom. Was it the mention of the South?

"How do you know all of this?" Kayleesh asked, her violet eyes sparkling.

"We have geologists and prospectors stationed on Truxxe; we have specialist equipment, scientists, mathematicians working out the quantities. It's no longer guesswork"

"And so why did you need us?"

"A fresh approach is always desirable – as is enthusiasm and gall. A lot of the other theorists in that meeting room are beyond retirement age – they lack the tenacity and drive of their younger years."

Kayleesh seemed to accept this answer, her expression almost smug.

Before long, the travellers were boarding the ship once more. Tom, Kayleesh and Raphyl were soon strapped back into their seats. Raphyl's grin was as wide as his intellibelt was stretchy, but the anxiety suggested on the face of the Augtopian reflected Tom's own. Tom took a deep breath, tried to relax his clammy hands. The VDU opposite him presented a view of the municipal building. The impressive structure looked even more grandiose with bright spotlights emphasising it against the backdrop of the twilit sky. Suddenly the image of the grand edifice began to judder and Tom intuitively tightened his grasp on the arms of the flight chair. He braced himself and it was all the strength he could muster not to shout out. Eyes screwed shut and teeth clenched, Tom rode out the take-off. The timepiece must have been bleeping again throughout his anxiety, but the sound of the ship's engines muffled the alarm. Once they were airborne, Tom recovered more quickly than he had the first time, but the relief still washed through him like a burst dam. Heart hammering and forehead perspiring, he took a deep breath.

"Woooh!" Raphyl exclaimed with joy. "You can't beat that!" Tom didn't respond and instead fixed his gaze on the white bands of light on the VDU which he knew to be stars. The door hummed open. Hyganty appeared, a tray of refreshments held delicately in his pincers. Tom was relieved to discover that it contained nothing which looked too strange.

After they had finished their meal and when Tom's guard was low, the Submian ship made an unexpectedly rough landing. Tom looked at his friends for reassurance. Kayleesh looked a little staggered, but Raphyl was licking hanaken sauce off his fingers as though the jolt had been the intensity of a mere speed bump.

"Seems like we've landed," Raphyl grinned. They followed the Submians through the ship, down the ramp and onto alien soil once more, ALSID bot between them. The first thing which Tom noticed was that it was daylight here. This felt strange to him having left the dusky desert of Hushgah what felt like mere hours previous. But it was more than daylight. It was inexorably bright. Tom soon discovered why.

"Ah, the beauty of Luenia," sighed Frarkk. "Much of this planet is currently in a state of perpetual daylight thanks to its binary star system. It revolves once around one sun and then once around the second," Frarkk drew the path of an infinity loop in the air with a feeler to demonstrate this. "And thus begins the cycle again."

"Must be hard to get any shut eye this time of year," Tom commented, half to himself. He looked up, shielding his eyes with one arm. There were indeed two suns in view. One appeared twice the size of the other and both just in his field of vision as he stood facing away from the spacecraft. He wondered if the planet was currently nearer the larger sun or whether it was simply bigger. It was certainly very warm here. The second thing Tom noticed was that he felt very light on his feet. He considered that the planet was either markedly smaller or less dense than he was used to. Frarkk was right – it *was* a beautiful planet. A breeze cooled Tom's face from the direction of a lake to the east of them. A wooded area ran round its south bank. Grass, with flat ochre stems grew beneath their feet. Tom could hear a faint sound akin to birdsong in the air. As the three of them readily followed the Submians, ALSID bot in tow, Tom realised that the birdsong was in fact the language of the Luenians. He was amused by the smooth transition of the whistling chatter into plain English as the orators came within their range. He was surprised to discover that the inhabitants looked very unlike birds, however. Dark red in colour and in cream dress, these bipeds stood ten feet proud. One or two of them were walking on their tiny feet using large, muscular tails to balance their lofty physiques which they swayed majestically as they advanced. Tom noticed a group who were gathered in conversation. They each had their strong tails coiled around their feet (obscuring their feet completely from view) helping them to remain steadfast and tall. Their small group approached the conversing beige and red crowd. Tom turned to Kayleesh.

"Don't tell me – the Submians want to attend another meeting!" he whispered. Kayleesh giggled. But it seemed that Hyganty was merely asking the Luenians for directions. Tom winced at the returned discomfort his injured leg was causing him, despite the decreased pressure on it from his reduced bodyweight. The thought of a painful trek wasn't a welcome one.

"Do you have any more of those fastacs?" he asked Raphyl.

Raphyl nodded and handed him the remainder of the packet. Tom freed one and swallowed it, benefiting from the instant relief. He was now prepared for the journey. However, there was little journey to be made as the lip of the crater was not far from their landing site, albeit partly obscured by woodland. *The Submians can find one planet in a whole galaxy universe of worlds, but they needed instructions on how to find a huge crater fifty feet from the ship.* The crater appeared to be of the same dimensions of the one in which Tom had found himself on Hushgah. From the rim of the great hollow, they observed as Hyganty leapt graciously down to observe the properties of the base. He soon returned, skin-tight garments glistening in the persistent sunlight. *He can't be very comfortable in those,* Tom thought. He was sweating in his own clothes.

"The ground has been scorched," Hyganty reported. "It's been subjected to the same intense heat as the crater on Hushgah. If you notice, the width and depth of the chasm match the other one." He waved a pincer demonstratively. Tom nodded. Kayleesh nodded also and grinned widely.

"Where's the machine, Hyganty? The one which they think relates to the crater formation?" she asked enthusiastically.

"Let's have a look shall we?" suggested Frarkk. A large ochre coppice ran along the path ahead of them as they followed the edge of the crater. They had to weave amongst bracken and trees as they progressed. Tom was grateful for the parasol-like quality of the shade offered by some of the larger trees. The terrain proved to be a problem for the ALSID bot, which kept bumping off tree roots and taking short flights in the minimal gravity before crashing back down to the ground. So Hyganty picked it up for ease and carried effortlessly under one arm as he had done so before. The group stopped once to replenish the fuel tank with glow rocks. Other than that, their movement was steady. A short while later, Tom again heard the natural birdcall voice of the Luenians. However, in contrast to the melodic babble he had heard earlier on, the sounds were harsh, staccato shrills. The voices transposed into recognisable tongue as they neared and Tom realised that one of the Luenians was shouting.

"Do not come any closer!"

# CHAPTER 20

"You are prohibited from passing through here!" she shouted, angrily. The Luenian was dressed in a dark brown coverall and wore a hard expression on a weathered face. Her arms were crossed boldly across her slender torso. Alarmingly, a gigantic, husky tail was coiled tightly around her base, like a crimson, concrete-like snake; solid and resolute. Her feet were completely obscured by the trunk-like tail. There were eight or ten other natives, dressed in beige, wearing the same expression – a wall of defiance. Peeking above this red wall, Tom could make out a pulsating green glow. Was this the *machine?*

"We've come a long way to survey the area," Hyganty said, bravely, pulling himself up on his insect-like legs to his full height.

"You have no business here. Turn back!"

"What are you hiding?" asked Hyganty.

"This is our business. You have no right to come here. Turn back!"

"We only want to look – we have not come to interfere in your affairs."

"You have already begun to interfere, Submian. Leave now and we will grant you safe passage.

Hyganty had no choice but to nod and take a step back. He turned to Tom and the others, resignedly.

"Let's go back to the ship."

It was obvious that the Submians were a peaceful people. But Tom couldn't help but feel disappointed.

"So, are we going back to Truxxe, then?" asked Raphyl. They were sitting on the bridge of the ship. It was markedly less comfortable than the luxurious passenger suite.

"Of course not, we just need to devise a plan," said Hyganty. Frarkk looked as though he was deep in thought.

"I wonder what secret they're hiding," pondered Kayleesh. "Do you think they're out there guarding the machine all the time, or did they know we were coming?"

"That wall of guards did seem a bit overkill to be there all the time," speculated Tom. "You'd think they'd have some kind of physical barricade around it instead. Maybe with a couple of guards patrolling. Either that or they could hide it better. The beacon of glowing green light is a bit of a giveaway."

"True," agreed Kayleesh.

"In that case we'll need to go unnoticed on our next attempt," said Frarkk, rather unnecessarily.

"I suppose asking for directions to the crater didn't do us any favours last time," Tom laughed. "We weren't exactly discreet!" Kayleesh and Raphyl laughed too, but the Submians remained staid.

"Couldn't we fight our way through? They're only reedy things," considered Raphyl.

"Have you seen the size of those tails, Raphyl?" Kayleesh gasped. "They're like tree trunks! Besides, we're outnumbered. And I don't like violence."

"We need to find another way round. And a decoy," said Frarkk.

"But they know there are five of us. If fewer than five confront them, they'll know that the remainder will be attempting to get through another way," Hyganty reflected. "They'll be prepared."

"Let's sleep on it. We should wait until their guard is down a little," said Frarkk.

"It seems strange to go to sleep when it's still daylight out there," Kayleesh noted.

"If we wait for darkness we could be waiting for months," said Hyganty. "I'll show you to the guest quarters."

Tom lay awake in his allotted quarters which he was sharing with Raphyl. Raphyl was already asleep in his own bed, snoring softly. Tom was trying to think of a way around the problem - *literally* around it. And if they *did* get to this machine – what would it mean? Would it answer any of their questions? He realised that this was the first time he had encountered any hostility on any of the worlds he had visited, with the exception of Baff Bulken. He wondered how the Spotoon team were doing without him. He then wondered how his family was doing without him. He was glad that he had used the holoceiver and that he'd been able to contact them, even just for a few minutes, because he had never been so far away from home.

The holoceiver – that was it! That was how they were going to solve the problem! Tom wanted nothing more than to wake up Raphyl and blurt out his idea there and then, but he forced himself to get some sleep and wait until everyone was awake.

They were having breakfast on the bridge of the Submian ship. It consisted of flat pieces of tasteless protein and some manner of vegetable served on dayglo plastic plates. Tom was trying to convince his taste buds that he was eating a tasty rasher of bacon with tomato. It wasn't working.

"So, you have an idea then, Tombo?" Raphyl asked, taking a huge bite of the flat protein.

"Yes. It might work." Tom was glad of the opportunity to stop eating while he spoke. His taste buds were dying of boredom. "Hyganty, is there anyone back on Truxxe who knows about this mission?"

"Yes, as I said before, there are people stationed all over."

"At TSS?"

"Yes."

"Great. Well, could we arrange for someone to use the holoceiver to remotely visit Luenia and have a look at the machine for us?"

Hyganty paused before responding. "Or better still – how about we arrange for a decoy to use the holoceiver and we can go and have a look ourselves?"

"One problem," Kayleesh said. "There's a waiting list for the holoceiver isn't there? It'd have to be booked days in advance."

Tom's heart sank. They didn't have days.

"TSS is not that only place you can call from. It's not the only holoceiver in the galaxy," Frarkk pointed out, a glint in his large, dark insectoid eye. He pressed a button on his timepiece and spoke into it "Larn? You're needed – one moment everyone." He proceeded to pace around the bridge apparently explaining the strategy to the potential decoy.

"Is that definitely the last of the gems cleared?" Schlomm had been contacted via holoceiver once again by his brother.

"Yes, the gem crystals we supplied in the meat must have all been processed because we haven't seen any more for rotations. Eto has been smuggling them out periodically. We must have thousands of them by now."

"And this Strellion – I suppose he'll want paying for his labour and secrecy?"

"He did mention wanting a cut, certainly, but it is a small price to pay for his efforts. I have managed to convince him that as the "founder" of the first gem I will take the highest percentage,"

"And he was happy with that?" asked Schlomm, almost as though he cared. He felt the situation too good to be true.

"He seemed content enough, yes."

"Strellions are such dumb beings, for all their curiosity and ponderings," Schlomm muttered. "All right, contact me again once you are ready for collection."

Tom Bowler, Kayleesh, Raphyl and the two Submians were making their way towards the place where the machine was being so heavily guarded. They were approaching it from the opposite direction this time. The path had proved much more arduous than their previous journey, however, and Tom was relieved to see a glimmer of shiny metal eventually glistening through the branches of the thick, ochre woodland. The relentless heat of the perpetual sunlight had fatigued the party quickly and even Hyganty, who had been carrying the ALSID bot so effortlessly at the start of the jaunt, was now showing signs of lethargy. Muscles aching and brows gleaming with perspiration, they came to a halt. Frarkk spoke softly into his timepiece.

"Larn? What's your location?"

"My projection has materialised twenty metres or so away from the machine," came the stifled reply. "I'm currently hiding my hologram behind a tree. There appear to be three guards."

"Thanks, Larn," whispered Frarrk. "And good luck."

"What is Larn going to say to them?" Raphyl asked.

"It doesn't matter – as long as he distracts them for long enough," said Frarrk. "I suppose he may be able to get some information from them, if he's cunning enough in his approach - being the curious Strellion that he is - but a diversion is all I've asked of him."

At Hyganty's lead, the group ventured forward. Wordlessly they progressed, the sound of breaking branches beneath their feet, the only sound. Presently they reached the large mechanism, a glowing, green sphere, twelve-foot in diameter. On closer inspection, beneath a lattice of green laser beams, Tom could see a black and infinitely smooth inner sphere. Tiny mirrors were redirecting the beams which constructed the geodesic network. They were very conscious that the guards were only the other side of the device and slowed their movements. Tom ran his eyes over the unfamiliar motionless, faceless machine. He tried to decide what it could be used for but there was little to go on. It seemed to him that the workings were chiefly hidden within the dark globe. What was its importance here on Luenia? The instrument was impressive, certainly, and the Submians were in apparent awe of the thing. Suddenly a flash of red and beige came into view. Tom's heart leapt in fear. Three angry Luenians, their hard faces pictures of pure rage glared at the five trespassers.

"We asked you politely to leave this area and *not come back,*" one of them spat. "And now I hear that you have not heeded our warning!" *And now he hears?* Thought Tom. *Who told him? Larn? He was supposed to be acting as a diversion.*

"I can see that you are shocked, Submian," the Luenian snarled at Frarrk. "You didn't think you could trust a *Strellion* did you? They are renowned liars. Mischief-makers. They make you believe that they are on your side – that they are compliant and willing to be *used*. When in truth they are using you for their own end. Or for their own amusement, at least," the Luenian seemed to be speaking from personal recollection, with undertones of loathing and resentment. "You made a misguided decision, Submian." The three guards uncoiled their muscular tails from around their steadfast stance in unison. Tom didn't wait to see what they were going to do next and instinctively grabbed Kayleesh's hand.

"Run!" They scrambled through thickets and bracken and across unstable undergrowth. Tom wasn't sure whether the others were hurrying behind them or whether they had managed to get away at all, but he could hear the shrill cries of timepiece beacons, detonated by raised heartrates, chiefly his own.

"Ssh!" he willed at the contraption around his wrist. The device was proving to be detrimental to the situation. The Luenians would surely follow the sound of the alarm. Annoyed, he tapped the timepiece hard against his leg in an attempt to cease its wailing. It worked. "Turn off your timepiece, Kayleesh," he told her. But Kayleesh didn't respond. *Hyganty has the ALSID bot,* he realised. Tom was so engaged with predicament in which they had found themselves, that he didn't notice the hole.

Tom shrank a full foot as his bad foot plummeted through the undergrowth. He swore in pain and frustration. Kayleesh almost tumbled to the floor with him but managed to slip from his grasp. She looked at him, but Tom couldn't read her expression. Her violet eyes looked beautifully terrifying. As she spoke her entire face seemed to resonate. Sounds were emitting from her mouth, low and soft, but they were nonsensical to Tom without the aid of an ALSID. He sat back on the rim of the hole, massaging his throbbing foot. Kayleesh was pointing and gesturing, but Tom looked up at her blankly. Then she turned and ran, timepiece squealing and flashing beyond the trees. He called fruitlessly after her. Had she gone to get help? Had she expected him to follow? Did she have a plan? Struggling to his feet he took the fastac pack out of his pocket and swallowed two. Readying himself to run after her he felt something on his shoulder. It was a hand. A red hand.

Tom's breath caught in his throat. His timepiece began to bleep once more, reacting to his body's responses. If he hadn't been frozen to the spot in fear, Tom was sure that he would have ripped the thing off and stamped on it there and then. Instead he gulped, and simply stared up into the wide-eyed Luenian who held him in his grasp. Tom was surprised when the grasp loosened and the stony look on that austere face softened. He was surprised further still that he could understand the being when he spoke.

"Don't worry – I'm not like the others. Quick, I'll hide you."
It took several moments before Tom was able to speak.
"OK," he said simply and followed the towering, crimson Luenian back the way he had ran and into a shallow hollow. Covered almost completely by leaves and branches, the two crouched and caught their breath. Tom's timepiece was silent once more. He wasn't sure whether he could trust him, but he didn't know what else to do. Would it be safer to try and escape his company and risk the others being alerted? He didn't think so.

"How come I can understand you?" he asked, eventually.
"I'm an interpreter – I know thousands of languages," he replied rather complacently.
"Even English?"
"It's more common than you'd think."
"Oh."

The Luenian spoke before Tom could probe further. "My name is Cass Harble," he extended a hand, congenially. Tom shook it. Cass seemed amiable enough.

"Tom Bowler."

"As I was saying, Tom, I'm not like the others – the guardians, with all their secrets and schemes."

"Secrets?"

"Yes, like the huge one you and your friends are trying to uncover."

"Do *you* know what the machine is for?" Tom asked, excitedly. He would find out and impress Kayleesh with his knowledge – he was better at this than those Submians.

"I know what it *was* for, yes," Cass whispered, coal-black eyes shining amid a coarse, rugged complexion. Despite the weathered quality to his skin, Tom suspected that Cass was not much older than himself. "Why they don't destroy it I don't know – it would be easier than all the paranoia and secrecy which goes along with preserving it! They are nothing but bigoted show-offs!"

"What was the machine built to do? Is it connected with the crater?"

"If anyone finds out I'm having this conversation with an alien, I'll be in a lot of trouble," Cass looked a little worried. Tom was taken aback at the term *alien* being used to describe himself. It rather amused him too.

"Well if you don't want to take the risk…" Tom began, although the last thing he wanted was for Cass to stop here. Cass shook his head and seemed almost human for a moment, in his mannerisms.

"The truth needs to be told," he asserted. Nevertheless, he took the trouble to peek out of the hollow to check for anyone who might be lurking around outside their hiding place. "The original purpose of all the other machines was to generate wormholes for instant space travel," he said in a low voice. "They were built independently of each other, by different races of advanced beings on different worlds." Tom nodded. He'd read about wormholes and the theory that they tear holes in space/time and link two places together. He was impressed that this had apparently been achieved and on such a great scale. He let Cass continue. "The Lueanians – my ancestors - were terrified of the prospect of this technology. They were primarily spacecraft manufacturers – an invention which could fold space and therefore make spacecrafts obsolete would be disastrous to our economy, so... and this is where it gets nasty... the Lueanians invented *this* machine, the Portal Re-router." Cass sighed. He looked almost ashamed, but Tom could sense the anger in his voice. "The PR was built to divert anything which was intended to be transported by re-routing the path. So, anyone attempting to travel through a wormhole wouldn't reach their destination – they would instead arrive at a default position. Therefore, the wormhole machines would be seen to be unsuccessful and the threat to the manufacture and use of spaceships would disappear. Which is exactly what happened."

"Clever – I think," said Tom. "What happened to the people who tried to use the wormhole travel then? Weren't they angry when they arrived at this *default position* rather than their destination? Could they get back to their own planets again?"

Cass lowered his eyes. "None of the travellers would have had a chance to survive," he paused, swallowed and then continued. "You see, the PR was so powerful that not only did it transport the traveller – it transported a great chunk of surrounding landmass with them... several hundred tonnes of rock would not be the best travelling companion. It wouldn't have been the softest of landings. This destruction was another reason for people to cease using their wormhole technology – it made the scheme so much more elaborate." Cass made eye contact with Tom for the first time since he had begun talking. There was a great sorrow in his eyes. Tom gulped at the prospect of all those deaths. Cass waved an arm in the direction of the crater. "The crater here was a test site – my ancestors wanted to check that the PR was powerful enough." Things were starting to piece together for Tom now. The size of the crater here matched the one on Hushgah because it had been created by the same means. *Such needless destruction.* He wondered how many other planets had mastered wormhole technology – how many chunks of terrain had been unnecessarily ripped out – and not just deserts and forests – how many towns and cities? *How many people?*

"And is all this still going on?" Tom tried not to get angry – Cass was a Lueanian, but he was no more responsible than Tom was for war in the Middle East.

"No, once it was known as a universal "fact" that the experiments were a failure, scientists just stopped trying. The machine is no longer in use – they brought it back here though as a kind of monument to their own secret success. They guard it like some kind of capitalistic trophy," he said, bitterly.

"Then where was the machine stationed before?"

"At the default position; on Truxxe."

# CHAPTER 21

Tom gasped. *Of course. It all makes sense.* Why hadn't he figured this out before? He was sure that one of the Submians must have pieced it together. Or perhaps Kayleesh.

Kayleesh – was she all right?

"I need to find the others," said Tom, focussing.

"Are you going to tell them?" Cass asked, warily.

"I'm going to have to – we came out here on a mission to discover the truth behind Truxxe – and now I have our answer. Me, a human - with all this information. It's big news. Huge! I'm not looking forward to telling Raphyl that half of his planet isn't Truxxian soil and that it's the result of… anyway, do you think it's safe to go out there yet?"

Cass listened for a moment.

"Yes, I think so. I'll hide here a little longer – it wouldn't be a good idea for me to be seen talking with you." Tom nodded, thanked Cass for the valuable information and ducked out of the hollow. He decided to make use of his timepiece. The symbols on it were indecipherable, as expected, but he punched at it haphazardly and spoke into it.

"Kayleesh? Raphyl? Are you near?"

"Tom, we've discovered something!" came Kayleesh's voice. "Make your way back round the crater and come back to the ship." What had they discovered? Tom felt almost disappointed – he had wanted to impress them all with his own news.

Hot and weary from the return journey, Tom tramped up the battalion green ramp, boots ringing on the metallic flooring. He found his way to the bridge where the others were seated, the ALSID bot resting between them. There was a face amongst the party which he didn't recognise; a Lueanian who was casually supping dark liquid from a glass. The ever-hospitable Submians seemed to have made this habitant feel quite at home on their ship already. After his friendly exchange with the kindly Cass, Tom wasn't frightened at the sight of the Lueanian. He took a seat.

"Tom, this is Smiker Harble," Kayleesh told him.

"Harble? I've just spoken to *Cass* Harble," said Tom.

"Then you've met my brother," Smiker said with a smile. He lifted his glass rather clumsily to his mouth. His mannerisms were not reminiscent of those of his brother – this Lueanian seemed a lot less refined and acted as though he had spent less time around other cultures as the inter-worldly-wise translator. He seemed less sure of himself and he was constantly examining his surroundings as though it were his first time aboard a spacecraft. Tom could relate to that feeling.

"Did he help you Tom?" Kayleesh asked, a look of relief on her face.

"Yes, he hid me until it was safe enough for me to come back."

"Smiker helped us too – I don't think we would have made it back here safely without him."

Tom nodded respectfully at Cass' brother. He wanted to tell Kayleesh and the others what Cass had told him in the hollow. But Hyganty was next to speak.

"Smiker has been helpful, two-fold. Not only has he been our protector, but he has provided us with information."

"About the machines and the Portal Rerouter?" Tom wanted to get a few words in – even if they weren't entirely fresh to the assembly. He wanted to prove that he wasn't just a pitiable human who was a burden to the group – that he was as capable of discovering things as any Submian, Truxxian or Augtopian. His few words had the desired effect on Kayleesh. He saw her smile, clearly impressed. He felt himself flush a little.

"Yes," Hyganty continued. "The PR was built to divert the travellers to a default position – ingenious technology I must admit. Cruel and self-centred, but ingenious all the same."

"You were about to tell us all how the Lueanians achieved it," Raphyl piped up, wide eyes fixed on Smiker. He had the same childlike look about him as when he had enthused about rocket-powered thrusters. Smiker took a final gulp of his drink, most of which sloshed down his chin, and remained there on account that it did not occur to the Lueanian to wipe it off. He began.

"The matrix of laser beams around the PR detect the most minute distortions caused by the creation of a wormhole in the neighbouring galaxies. Once activated via this detection circuit, the smooth sphere which has a negative gravitational effect lifts the PR to the pinnacle of space/time. Once the PR has reached the pinnacle, the secondary inner sphere is activated which has a positive gravitational force which pulls the PR down to the bottom of space/time through a narrow gravity well. Therefore, anything which is attempting to travel through a wormhole is pulled down the central gravity well and to the location of the PR. The distortion created by the PR in space/time would resemble a volcano, but on a galactic scale."

Hyganty nodded, slowly. "So, it would be like drilling through the side of a volcano and instead of reaching the magma core, you would get pulled into the core. The force would be so great that there would be a direct link"

"Exactly. The power of the PR is immense and therefore able to drag through the geology of the planet in question."

"Is the PR machine on all the time?" Tom asked.

"Of course not, the energy requirements would be too great," Smiker said. "The control circuit in the centre switches off after mere nanoseconds. Then the detection lattice resets and continues to monitor for wormhole activity."

"It looks as though the machine is still activated," Kayleesh pointed out.

"Yes, the lattice is still running (the control circuitry is faulty after aeons of use), but as wormhole technology has been quashed, there is no fear that the lattice would be triggered."

Tom gulped.

"Hyganty, I wanted to ask," Tom asked later, before leaving the bridge for his quarters. "How come you didn't figure any of this out before? I mean, the PR machine was here all along, there are Lueanians who would obviously been willing to join your conspiracy theorist group, willing to give you all the answers and…"

"Tom, the universe is a very big place," he replied, rather condescendingly, Tom thought. "Besides, there are a lot of Strellions amongst us – a species we Submians shall never trust again. We have been led on many a wild grooble chase these past few solar years which are undoubtedly down to those troublemakers! Without the "help" of that race I believe we would have come across the answer a lot more quickly."

"Er… Schlomm?"

"What is it Hannond? Have all the gems been gathered?" came the eager response.

"Y… yes but there is a… problem," stuttered Hannond's nervous hologram.

Schlomm looked accusingly at his brother's image which was being projected once more aboard the Cluock.

"A *problem?*" His voice turned sour.

"Eto has shifted all the gems as we planned."

"Good, good…"

"But,"

"But?"

Hannond dared to continue. He felt his short throat tighten; his perspiration glands began to excrete until his stubby grey hands felt the sweat of fear. He knew how Schlomm was going to react, but there was no way of avoiding this conversation. Despite the refuge of the holoceiver skin, Schlomm's virtual proximity disconcerted him. He began, softly,

"I haven't seen Eto for several rotations and… and… I'm not *entirely* sure where he said he was storing the gems. In fact, I'm not sure he ever told me…"

"*What?*" Schlomm boomed. "You're saying that you entrusted the Strellion with *our gems* and you didn't even think to ask him where he was storing them?"

"I'm sorry, I… I didn't think that… I was so excited that… I was so busy retrieving them that it didn't occur to me that…"

*"That that that!"* Schlomm mocked, teeth dripping with acrid saliva. "It didn't occur to you that he was *stealing* them from us? I knew you were idiotically trusting, *dear brother,* but I didn't think you were so naïve!" his voice softened to a maddening whisper. "There is no way to describe the anger I have for you right now Hannond, I'm afraid that I'm going to have to leave you there because if I see you in person, I will shove a Glorbian gem so far up your… aagh!" he growled in frustration and wrath. "I don't even *have* one gem to perform the action! After all our hard work! I can't believe this," he growled again, with such force that it almost caused the ship to shake. Schlomm's anger was so apparent that the cowering image of Hannond could almost see the inferno of hatred for him in his eyes. He backed away, pleading for his holoceiver session to be terminated.

Suddenly, Schlomm advanced on him, hairy fingers and thumbs outstretched, preparing to strangle him. Hannond knew that this was impossible of course, in his yellow-tinged bubble, but as his consciousness faded back to the TSS holoceiver booth, he couldn't help but let out a pained scream.

# CHAPTER 22

When Tom opened his eyes he had the inexplicable gut feeling that they had changed location and were no longer on Lueania. Were they in flight or had they landed on some other distant world? Tom vacated the room and found the others on the bridge once more. Kayleesh smiled warmly at him.

"We're home, Tom."

"Home?"

"Yes, back at TSS."

"Oh, right," Tom ran his fingers through his mass of bed-head hair. He felt a little disorientated. "I don't remember taking off – surely I didn't sleep through that?"

"I remember the intellibelts securing me in place in my bed just before take-off – I was still awake but yes, you must have slept through it, then. I'm impressed!"

"So am I!" exclaimed Tom.

Tom realised that he hadn't had a bath in a long time and was feeling uncomfortable in the same compsuit. Kayleesh looked as fresh as ever in her TSS uniform, however, and Tom liked simply looking at her. Raphyl, Hyganty and Frarkk were wearing the visions of dark jeans and hooded tops as portrayed by their compsuits. *We definitely must be back on Truxxe.*

"How long do we have until our weekend - I mean free days - are over?" Tom asked Raphyl casually as they disembarked the ship.

"Er, we were away a little longer than you think, Tombo," he laughed.

"What do you mean? It couldn't have been that long - we've slept, what, twice?"

"And how far have we travelled? Warping space/time and travelling at those speeds across the galaxy means we've aged more than everyone who's remained here the whole time."

"Exactly *how much* time has passed?" his response from Raphyl as an infuriating guffaw. "Kayleesh?"

"Er…" she tried to be sensitive in the delivery of her answer. "About four months," she bit her lip.

"*Four months?*" Tom stopped dead in the middle of the spaceport. This was certainly the longest he had gone without a bath. "Won't we get fired?"

"No, the employers here are used to this happening all the time – as long as you realise we won't get paid for those four months, of course."

"More importantly," came a deep voice from his left. It was Ghy Hasprin. "You've missed a hell of a lot of Spotoon practice – the big match is tomorrow." He cocked his ear in his direction. "Glad to have you home!"

The following day, Tom was back working behind the counter at the TSS Express Cuisine restaurant. He felt refreshed after a long spell in the bathroom of his apartment and a long sleep. He was both excited and apprehensive about the impending evening's big match. He had been sorry to have missed the hype and build-up of the imminent game but at the same time he felt relieved that he hadn't felt the swelling pressure of the previous weeks as experienced by his team-mates. He was feeling the pressure today though. He hadn't had nearly as much practice as his team-mates and he didn't know how fierce the competition might be. After practice with Hasprin's Legion on his return to Truxxe the previous evening, he had learned that the match was to be held at an arena on the ground floor of the station. Tom knew that this meant that the spectators would consist of hundreds of visitors to the complex and not just the employees who resided in the upper floors and frequented bar six-seven. Hasprin's Legion were up against five other professional teams; one of them being the BBs. Tom cringed at the thought of the sweaty oaf that was Baff Bulken. If Baff made him nervous enough, perhaps he would vomit on him again in self-defence. *I wonder if that's in the rules,* he thought. The lit segments on his timepiece made their slow progression to the fifth hour when Tom could leave his post. As the fifth segment lit, however, Tom felt a compelling notion to remain where he was. His supervisor, Miss Lolah, had bumbled up to him on her brass, barely humanoid legs.

"We are one person down for the first hour of the twilight shift," came the soft, deeply feminine voice from that factory-floor grille. "Tom, I wonder whether you would be so kind as to work overtime until the sixth hour." Her voice filtered through his mind like molten butterscotch drizzled on ice cream. The lens on her polished face clicked and whirred.

He was transfixed, unable to prevent his response from being anything other than,

"Yes." The lubberly, lumpish Miss Lolah turned away and headed towards the staff room. A cross Augtopian remained – Kayleesh glared at him.

"Tom, what are you doing? The match is at the seventh hour, you can't work late tonight! Tonight, of all nights!"

"I had no choice, Kayleesh. You know how she works," he replied glumly. Kayleesh shook her head in disbelief. The hour crawled by, but the moment the latecomer arrived to relieve him of his duties, Tom was ready to make his way to his apartment to change out of his uniform. He left the restaurant, turned the corner and was met by Kayleesh. She was holding a compsuit.

"You haven't got time to go back to your room – why don't you get changed in the staff room? Here, you can borrow my spare." Her violet eyes were smiling, her elfin face framed perfectly by her golden hair. He grinned gratefully at her and took the compsuit.

Kayleesh and Raphyl were waiting outside the staff room when Tom emerged. Kayleesh's compsuit felt comfortable – it had adapted to his body shape like his own. The three of them walked through the bustling maze of the service station, the disquietude Tom felt increasing with every step. The foreboding sense of apprehension he felt was not helped the escalating number of people who seemed to be walking in the same direction – were they all going to watch the match? How popular was the sport here? Was it one of many or was this the main event of the season? He hoped that he played well tonight. Signs for the arena were pointing towards the far end of a passageway which Tom had not been down before. The passageway widened, but the density of pedestrians did not decrease for there were so many people heading in the same direction. Soon the avenue opened into an extensive space lined with seats; the arena lay before them. Tom gaped. He realised that they were being involuntarily carried in the current of the crowd towards the seating area.

"Tom!" Ghy's voice was faint but recognisable. Where was he? All Tom could see was a multicoloured blur of alien beings all around him. A heavy burgundy hand landed on his shoulder, pulling him in the opposite direction. He let his feet follow and eventually found himself out of the swell of the crowd – and in the centre of the arena. "Players sit over there," Ghy told him, shouting above the crowd. He pointed at three long benches at the opposite end of the pitch. "Let's take the direct route." Tom walked right across the arena with Ghy, who was lumbering along on his four strong forearms. They passed the Spotoon board in the centre, which was positioned onto a post – a mere raisin in the centre of the dining table of a stadium, by comparison. They joined their fellow team-mates on the second row of the ergonomic players' benches. Tom sat down and the immediate vicinity of the bench's form twisted and softened into shape for his use. Ghy lowered his bulky torso next to him, his part of the bench pulsing upwards to meet his tall and hefty frame and supporting his four limbs. Tom saw that there were vast screens all around the arena, all focussed on the oche. Tom gulped. There were a lot of people who were going to have their eyes on those huge screens; watching his spittle, enlarged to ten-feet tall, shoot out of his mouth and onto that board. They would surely be able to see the beads of perspiration on his brow, detect his anxiety and his quickened pulse. How he wished he were merely spectating rather than participating. He wiped his clammy hands on his compsuit - on Kayleesh's compsuit, he realised. He wondered where she and Raphyl were sitting. He had no hope of being able to spot them among the heaving mass of the audience.

By the seventh hour, the influx of beings had slowed to a trickle as the last of the seats were filled. A voice boomed, resounding and incorporeal.

"Welcome to the nineteenth Spotoon match!" it announced. The crowd roared so loudly that Tom's instinct was to cover his ears, but then he saw his own face, as large as a house projected on the multitude of screens lining the stadium. In the edge of his vision he saw Ghy angle his protruding ear towards him. A smile broke out on Tom's face and he copied the gesture, for the crowd to see. The volume of the cheering amplified two-fold; his confidence soared. "This is the rundown of the teams we have battling for the giant Glorbian gem-stone trophy tonight," the disembodied voice began.

"We have The Gharka," there were rousing cheers amongst the crowd; "The BBs" more cheering and a few hundred boos; "Aykiera's Army," more cheering; "Hasprin's Legion," more cheering, particularly in his right ear which Tom felt would never work again thanks to his captain; "The Bornes", further cheering; "and of course last season's winners – "The Right

Ons." The arena gave rise to thunderous cheering and applause. Tom laughed to himself at the name of the last team. *The Right Ons?* They sounded like an eighties pop band. He stopped himself from laughing quickly, however - what if he was seen be mocking the team, his face fifty-feet high and repeated twenty times around the stadium? He didn't fancy his chances against their tremendous fan base. "The usual rules will apply tonight," the commentator continued. The crowd hushed a few decibels. "The first round will consist of three games, the two highest scoring teams will then compete against each other in the final round to decide who goes home with the trophy and the glory," the crowd roared momentarily. "The usual scoring system will be in place – go for the green, guys. And those of you who have the composition, go for green on green! Seriously though, teams, extra points will be awarded for style, vigour and power. So, if you can blast a hole through that disc, all the better. Good luck to you all! First up we have The Right Ons versus The Gharka!" the crowd exploded in applause, predictably. Tom was relieved that Hasprin's Legion was not one of the first teams to play – we wanted to get a feel for the match before he took a turn. He was rather enjoying the atmosphere now, despite his nerves. "The Gharka team captain Eto Straslond is unfortunately unable to play today," the commentator boomed as the two teams made their way to the centre of the arena. "Therefore, Hannond Putt will take his place as team captain and we will welcome fifth member Phelmer to make up the team." The crowd applauded politely. Phelmer? Tom couldn't imagine him playing Spotoon. *It must have been a last-minute decision. I wonder what happened to Eto?*

Tom watched the screen high up and opposite him, now that the two teams had become two indistinguishable lines on the pitch. Hannond Putt stepped up to the chalked line. The crowd fell silent. Those large, docile eyes in that coarse, leathery face oozed concentration. After a long pause, the short, stocky Glorbian lurched forwards and upwards and his dart of sputum flew through the air and scored The Gharka a green. He had obviously had a lot of practice since Tom had last seen him; enough to have been made captain. Next, a strangely tubby Truxxian from The Right Ons took his place at the oche and scored within the red ring. He had missed the green inner circle by millimetres, but the force of his shot had been impressive, and the crowd's reaction agreed with Tom's observation.

Perhaps the judges would take the effort into account for scoring, he thought. Once each of the teams had taken two turns, the commentator announced the judges' decision. The results were accompanied by a rousing fanfare produced by a sound Tom could only describe as discordant electronic bag pipes, and the flashing name of the winning team on the dozen or so screens, "The Right Ons". The crowd exerted itself, cheering and applauding once again as both teams returned to their benches. The disembodied voice announced the next round.

"Next up – Hasprin's Legion and…"

*Please not BBs, please not BBs.*

"…BBs." Jeers and cheers rose from the crowd Tom took a deep breath. Ghy stood up on his four muscular arms and pulled his burgundy body confidently towards the Spotoon board. Matey Reeston followed close behind, his lithe orange legs quickening their pace to keep up with the captain. Chazner and the pot-bellied Ransel looked round at Tom, gave an encouraging Hasprin's Legion signal in unison and waited for him to join them. With half reluctance, Tom followed the two Truxxians. He wanted to play, but he *really* didn't want to play against Baff Bulken and his team. He caught sight of each of their faces in turn on the screens, as the two teams advanced towards the centre of the arena. The fifty-foot vision of Baff's slavering, filthy features nigh on terrified him. *I'm so glad this is not a contact sport!*

Ghy stood proudly at the oche, brawny shoulders back, chest distended. He readied himself, punched one front fist into the other, paused and *ptoooo*, sent a wad of spit flying into… into the *orange* outer ring. This was not a good start. The commentator echoed Tom's thoughts. He could feel Baff's hot, rancid breath on his back, sense the glee at their misfortune. Then the creature brushed purposefully past Tom to take his turn. The green, rippling bulk of the grotesque captain breathed noisily and stood salivating as yellow saliva dribbled revoltingly through his matted brown facial hair like washing up liquid through a filthy wire soap pad. After a few snorts and grunts, he finally projected a cloudy torpedo of saliva at the board, scoring a sickeningly perfect green. The crowd reacted, a soup of cheers, jeers and boos. The vainglorious look in the competitor's eye was clear. The Truxxian Chazner stepped up next and calmly set himself up before scoring within the red ring. It was good, but not good enough to score, Tom feared. There was very little verve or vigour executed in the shot, despite the smooth delivery. The BB member who had hissed at Tom that night in Ghy's apartment was next, all tentacles and protrusions. Tom smiled inwardly as he failed to hit the board at all. *Baff's not going to be happy with that*, he thought, catching his expression. Ghy signalled Tom to take the next turn and his inner smile faded. Kayleesh was watching, Raphyl was watching, half of the galaxy was probably watching. *I wonder if this is being televised? What am I doing? Now calm down, Tom, just concentrate. Focus.*

He took several deep breaths and prayed that his timepiece wouldn't detect his nervousness and betray his calm exterior. Suddenly, he glimpsed Baff's heaving, salivating visage on the screens above the arena, felt the resentful glare from those tiny eyes. The image distressed him and knocked all concentration out of him, causing him to rush his turn. He managed a pathetic shot at the outer orange ring. A poor score and with half of the potency and power of Ghy's effort. Shaking his head in disappointment he vacated the oche, avoiding eye contact with his team-mates. A pitying cry from the crowd did nothing for his confidence. He could imagine the empathetic expression Kayleesh would be making at that moment and felt ashamed. Tom still didn't fully understand the scoring system, but it didn't take an expert to work out that he was not currently on the winning team as each of the other players took their turns. Hasprin's Legion was good, but not good enough.

When Ghy Hasprin's turn came round again, he strode up to the oche with more determination than ever, vowing to turn the game around. He took a shot and scored their highest score yet – the spittle landed directly in the centre of the green circle; he was back on form. Baff swaggered up to the line once more, his grotesque gait amplified by the viewing screens around them. His shot - most certainly full of anger at Ghy's victory – forced out his spittle with so much dynamism that it really did go straight through the disc, as the commentator had jested. Open mouthed, amid the crowd's cheers and the commentator's exclamations, the teams watched as a Truxxian, dressed in TSS blue, approached the post and replaced the disc with a fresh one. How could Tom possibly follow that? Baff knew that he couldn't and glared at him, more yellow drool flowing from his mouth. *Doesn't he ever run out of that stuff?*

Tom took his position, picturing Baff's vile, greasy face ahead of him in place of the new board. Tom drew up all the saliva he could muster and spat as hard and fast as he could at the disc. The crowd's reaction registered before his eyes could tell him that he had scored within the green zone. Feet lighter than air, he took his place back in line. He, Tom Bowler, an Earthling, had scored the second green for his team. He wanted to contain the feeling and treasure it; pure ego-ridden ecstasy. His team-mates gave an approving gesture, cocking their ears in his direction. His beaming face occupied the surrounding screens, but Tom wasn't embarrassed, he was proud. He was no longer the boy who was picked last for teams on the school football field, he was a champion. Well, almost. He hadn't quite blown a hole through the board, but it was a human impossibility and he was proud of his achievement all the same. This feeling stayed with him through the rest of the round. Although Chazner, Matey and Ransel played well, their score couldn't quite match those of the remainder of the BBs. All too soon the tuneless electronic bagpipes played their fanfare and the commentator pronounced the BBs to be the winners. Shoulders drooped and Tom followed his team-mates back to the ergonomic benches. The smugness which emanated from the winning team was sickening. Matey sat next to him and forced a grin which comically engaged his whole face.

"Don't worry, Tom, you played well. We all did – hey what's that?" Tom followed his gaze. He was looking up at one of the screens. The screen showed a black object held between lilac fingers; a five D piece. The Truxxian who had replenished the Spotoon board was stooped in the middle of the arena. Tom looked up at the screen again. He noticed that the coin was drenched in yellow saliva.

"It looks like we have a cheat in the arena in the shape of *Baff Bulken,*" came the accusatory boom of the commentator. "This counts as instant disqualification. Therefore, by default, Hasprin's Legion wins the round!"

# CHAPTER 23

Tom felt as though he was drowning in a sea of limbs.

"We did it, Tom. We beat BBs!" Matey Reeston exclaimed as he enthusiastically embraced the human.

"Does that mean we're through to the next round?" asked Tom.

"Not necessarily, it depends on who scores the highest of the three initial games," recapped Matey. "If the winner of The Bornes versus Aykiera's Army scores higher than us, then it will be them against the Right Ons. And whoever wins that round wins the whole match."

"I see. Hey, look, the BBs are being escorted out," Tom noticed.

They watched the next game with interest. Now that Baff's team were safely out of the way Tom felt much more relaxed and started to enjoy himself a bit more. He hoped that he'd get another chance to play today so that his confidence in himself and his enthusiasm for the game could grow. Soon enough the winning team was announced.

"The winners are… The Bornes!" The name danced triumphantly on the screens around them at the proclamation. Tom clapped and cheered along with the crowd and then listened intently for that vital piece of information. "The scores have been calculated. The Right Ons will play against… Hasprin's Legion!" Tom jumped to his feet in an almost involuntarily motion, his team-mates whooping and yelling joyously. "So join us in the second half."

"Don't we get to play now?" Tom turned to Matey, heart thumping so quickly with excitement that he had to remove his timepiece and put it in his pocket.

"Calm down, we'll be playing soon enough. We've got a few kroms yet. Looks like your friends have come to congratulate you," he said. Tom turned to see that Kayleesh had come running up to him, with Raphyl sauntering up behind her carrying a tray of drinks. He was taken aback by her sudden impulse to hug him. Wafts of her cinnamon-scented hair enveloped his senses.

"Well done, Tom. You got through to the final!"

"Only because BBs were disqualified," Tom said, modestly.

"You still got there honestly!"

Tom shrugged. "There's a good atmosphere here isn't there?"

"The best! And it's even better up here with all the teams." She looked around the players benches. "It's amazing. Hey, Raphyl's got us some drinks."

"Here you go, Tombo," Raphyl handed him a large plastic beaker. The contents smelled strongly of alcohol. He took a sip and coughed. Its strength warmed him. "You're playing well – well your second go was good anyway."

"Good? It was fantastic," Kayleesh grinned. Tom blushed and attempted to hide his shyness in his cup. Before Tom had barely finished his drink, his friends were making their way back to their seats and the commentator broke the intermission.

"Will Hasprin's Legion and the Right Ons please make their way to the oche?" Tom took a final swig and marched unquestioningly towards the Spotoon board with the others. The Right Ons captain was first to play. He was an Augtopian, like Kayleesh. He had lustrous brown waist-length hair and a determined look on his elfin face. His violet eyes narrowed as he prepared to take the first shot. He scored a perfect green. Ghy played next, scoring an equally matched point. A creature with centipedal legs and a body shaped like a strange parody of a concertina projected his pink sputum into the middle red ring. It was Tom's turn. Head held high, he convinced himself that he was confident and that he could score high again. He took his shot, then sucked hissing air back through his clenched teeth as he watched the globule land just short of the green circle. Not too disheartened, however, he watched a Truxxian on the opposing team take his turn. The lithe creature scored another perfect green with such gusto that it was bound to have been the highest scoring shot yet. The game was a close one, with both teams scoring within the green and red rings. On Tom's second go he managed to score within the green zone for the second time that day. Just as the round was reaching its conclusion, the announcer put the pressure on.

"Folks, this is the decider – the scores so far are exactly equal. The performance of the final two competitors will decide the overall score." Tom was grateful that this immense pressure wasn't on him, but felt for Chazner, who was last to play. Chazner nervously looked on as the Right Ons' final player composed himself. The insectoid being took his time, flexing his limbs needlessly and taking short, sharp breaths. The audience was muted. The atmosphere was tense. He made a series of curious noises in his throat and then suddenly spat with impressive force, sending a cloudy blob of mucus tearing toward the board. Green. The crowd stirred. Chazner, looking understandably overwrought, made his way to the chalked line. The Truxxian took his time, undoubtedly knowing that the next move was crucial – almost wanting to remain in this state of ignorant bliss, in case the result was not the one they required. He took his shot. As though in slow motion, the teams watched the progress of that bead of fluid. The audience fixedly watched the screens which portrayed the journey of the ten feet high wad. As it hit the red middle ring, the crowd detonated in an upsurge of cheers and woops at the triumph of the Right Ons. Those critical millimetres short of the green inner ring meant that Hasprin's Legion would not be taking home the trophy. Nevertheless, the team-mates gesticulated their notorious signal, left ears cocked, at the disheartened Truxxian. Tom was disappointed but gave him an amicable smile and went to congratulate the winning team.

That evening was spent celebrating the completion of the Spotoon season with their fellow teams. Tom was surprised at how warm the teams were toward each other, particularly over a sport which was seemingly taken rather seriously here. He was pleased to discover that the BBs had opted to not show up at Six Seven that night. He spent so much of the evening socialising with his team-mates and verbally re-living every second of the match that he realised he hadn't spoken to Raphyl since they had arrived. He found him sitting alone in the corner of the room, one eye half closed, contentedly concentrating on picking dirt out of his long fingernails and examining the resulting grime. He was looking rather inebriated and his words were slurred.

"So what happens now?" Tom asked.

"I'll jusht flick the dirt on the floor – I'm shure they won't mind," he said without looking up from his business.

"What? No, I mean, now that we know the truth about Truxxe, what happens? What do we do?" Raphyl shrugged.

"We carry on as normal, I guesh. Back to sherving those burgers."

"But what does it mean for the Truxxians?" Didn't Raphyl care about his home planet? "You're a Truxxian – aren't you bothered that half of your planet is a graveyard mishmash of diverted traffic?"

"Not really, it makesh no differensh to me in the long run because I know where I'm from – I'm still Truxshian." Raphyl absent-mindedly studied his fingernails once more, yawned deeply then rested his head on the table.

"I see…" Tom tried to see things from Raphyl's perspective. "It's because you're from the *southern* hemisphere that you know you were born on Truxxian soil?"

"Who said I was from the shouth? I'm not an immigrant from the shouth. I'm an immigrant from the pasht."

"From the *past?*" Tom gasped. "Raphyl? What do you mean?" But the only response he received was a loud snore.

# ALSO BY RUTH MASTERS

## THE TRUXXE TRILOGY

Three novels following the adventures of Tom Bowler, a human who finds himself working in an intergalactic service station during his gap year.

He discovers the secrets of the planetoid Truxxe, traverses the galaxy to rescue his alien friend from the prison planet Porriduum and ultimately defends the earth against an alien invasion.

A cast of colourful aliens good and bad, fantastic alien worlds and witty dialogue make this trilogy a great read for any sci-fi fan!

Vol 1: All Aliens Like Burgers
Vol 2: Do Aliens Read Sci-Fi?
Vol 3. When Aliens Play Trumps

## AUTOGRAPH HUNTER SERIES

A pair of "paraquels", each covering similar events, from the perspective of different characters.

In both books, attendees at the same sci-fi convention happen across a real working time machine, and set off on autograph-hunting missions through time.

The two pairs of friends cross paths occasionally, with Rosemary and Joanne intriguingly being one step ahead of Alistair and Jeremy.

Along the way they meet the great and the good of history, from Shakespeare to the inventor of the modern toilet. Friendships are tested and life will never be the same again…

Vol 1: Extreme Autograph Hunters
Vol 2: Ultimate Autograph Hunters

## BELISHA BEACON & TABITHA TURNER

Tabitha Turner is a complaints executive from contemporary Birmingham. Belisha Beacon is a celebrity DJ working on the illustrious Möbius Strip, orbiting the planet Hayfen IV, 400 years in the future.

Inexplicably finding themselves inhabiting each other's bodies and living each other's lives the two women must survive in a strange new world.

How will they get back to their own realities… and do they want to? Nothing is ever as it seems as Belisha and Tabitha's lives begin to change forever.

**Order from www.ruthmastersscifi.com or on Amazon.**

Printed in Great Britain
by Amazon